A New
Sun Rises
Over the
Old Land

T0083650

A New Sun Rises Over the Old Land

A NOVEL OF SIHANOUK'S CAMBODIA

SUON SORIN

Translated by Roger Nelson

NUS PRESS
SINGAPORE

Published by:

NUS Press
National University of Singapore
AS3-01-02, 3 Arts Link
Singapore 117569

Fax: (65) 6774-0652
E-mail: nusbooks@nus.edu.sg
Website: http://nuspress.nus.edu.sg

ISBN: 978-981-3250-77-2

National Library Board, Singapore Cataloguing in Publication Data

Names: Suon, Sorin. | Nelson, Roger (Art historian), translator, writer of introduction.
Title: A new sun rises over the old land : a novel of Sihanouk's Cambodia / by Suon Sorin ; translated and with an introduction by Roger Nelson.
Description: Singapore : NUS Press, [2019] | Includes bibliographic references. | Translated from Khmer.
Identifiers: OCN 1113445239 | ISBN 978-981-32-5077-2 (paperback)
Subjects: LCSH: Cambodia--History--1953-1975--Fiction. | Cambodians--Social conditions--Fiction. | Pedicab drivers--Cambodia--Fiction.
Classification: DDC 895.9323--dc23

Proceeds from the sale of this book will be paid to Sa Sa Art Projects, which is an artist-run space in Phnom Penh, which offers not-for-profit education, exhibitions, artists' residencies, and other community-oriented activities.

Front cover image: Merkushev Vasiliy/Shutterstock.com
Back cover image: Nhek Dim, c. 1960s. Reproduced with kind permission of Vandy Dim Nhek

Typeset by: Ogma Solutions Pvt Ltd
Printed by: Markono Print Media Pte Ltd

Table of Contents

Acknowledgements

Although modern Khmer literature has been comparatively little studied since its emergence in the late 1930s, historians have offered us rich accounts of Cambodia in this period leading to and following national independence, with a revealing emphasis on social and cultural transformations. Chief among these has been David Chandler, whose friendship and conversation I have had the privilege of enjoying. David's insights and advice have been invaluable, and I am very grateful to him for his generosity in sharing resources, reading and commenting on drafts of my writing, and supporting my work.

Since I am not Cambodian and Khmer is not my first language, my understanding of Khmer literature is also indebted to numerous friends and colleagues in Phnom Penh, with whom I have discussed the Khmer language, modern Khmer novels, and "Cambodian arts" more generally, as well as their relationships to the city and urban life, and to history. I thank them all, and especially Pen Sereypagna, Vuth Lyno, Khvay Samnang, and Tith Kanitha. My teacher, Chin Setha, who first introduced me to Suon Sorin and this novel, has been the finest guide to the Khmer language and to Cambodian Buddhism that I could ever hope to meet. I hope that this book brings him some happiness. Khing Hoc Dy, the preeminent expert in Khmer literature, has generously shared thoughts and resources, as have Christophe Macquet, Klairung Amratisha, Chairat Polmuk, and others. I am indebted to them all for their kindness and insights.

My understanding of Khmer literature grows from my research on other "Cambodian arts" of the twentieth and twenty-first centuries. I believe that paying attention to trans-media intersections within and between different forms of modern and contemporary arts is crucial to apprehending their historical importance, and their potential meanings. This book thus draws in part on my doctoral thesis on this topic. I am grateful to my doctoral examiners, Patrick D. Flores and Ashley Thompson, for their illuminating comments on that work, and for their provocations and contributions more broadly over several years. I also thank my doctoral supervisors at the University of Melbourne: Edwin Jurriens, Lewis Mayo, and Nikos Papastergiadis. I was fortunate to receive an Australian Postgraduate Award, as well as additional support from the University of Melbourne, in the form of an Asia Institute Scholarship, and a Graduate School of Humanities and Social Sciences Fieldwork Grant. Together, this financial assistance made this research possible.

This book was completed while undertaking a Postdoctoral Fellowship at Nanyang Technological University, Singapore, affiliated with the School of Art, Design and Media and the NTU Centre for Contemporary Art Singapore. I am very grateful for that opportunity, and for the support of colleagues at NTU, including at its libraries. Elsewhere in Singapore, T.K. Sabapathy has been a wise and generous friend and mentor. He was instrumental in bringing me to this island, and his conversations and vision have greatly enriched my time here. I also received valuable feedback on my approach to Khmer literature at a symposium on the subject of literary and artistic intersections in twentieth-century Southeast Asia, convened by Yin Ker and held at NTU. Final work on the preparation of this book was done after my appointment as Curator at National Gallery Singapore. I thank my wonderful colleagues there for their support.

Both the introduction and the translation have benefited from insightful comments and corrections from two anonymous peer reviewers. I thank them both for their diligence. All remaining errors are, of course, mine alone.

NUS Press has been a joy to work with on this book, as well as on the journal, *Southeast of Now: Directions in Contemporary and Modern Art in Asia*, which I co-founded and co-edit, and which they also publish. I thank them for their belief in these projects.

I thank Vandy Dim Nhek and Vuth Lyno for generously granting permission to reproduce the artworks of Nhek Dim and Pann Tra, respectively.

My final thanks are to my friends and family. In particular, I thank Anna Cordner, Dom Richardson, Simon Soon, Marion Campbell, Guo-Liang Tan, and Brandon Chua; as well as Danni Jarrett, Chris Roussos, Myrina and Georgia Roussos; and Edward and Pam Nelson. Most especially, I thank Liz Reed. This book is dedicated to her.

An Introduction

by Roger Nelson

First published in 1961, eight years after Cambodia gained independence from French colonial rule, *A New Sun Rises Over the Old Land* (*Brah Ādity Thmī Rah Loe Phaentī Cas*) by Suon Sorin is an iconic work of modern Khmer literature. A story of the hardships endured by a man who moves from the countryside to the city and finds work as a *cyclo* driver, the novel is also a singularly illuminating historical document of nationalist discourse in the new nation. The novel offers a previously unavailable view into a period of profound transformation in Cambodia, as in neighbouring countries. Concomitant with the processes of decolonisation, this was also a time when the region was coming to know itself and to be known as "Southeast Asia".

Sorin's novel offers a special insight into the contradictions and complexities inherent in the postcolonial regime called the Sangkum Reastr Niyum ("People's Socialist Community"), headed by Prince Norodom Sihanouk from 1955 to 1970.[1] The "Sangkum", as it is commonly known,

---

[1] I am deeply indebted to David Chandler—the preeminent Anglophone historian of Cambodia, who has worked on the country for more than half a century—for his generous support of my work here, and for his very insightful comments on an earlier draft of this introduction.

Unless otherwise noted, all translations are my own. I have followed the Library of Congress system for romanisation of Khmer, with some diacritical marks omitted, except for proper nouns, for which I have followed conventional spellings. Hence, for example, the author's name, *Suan Surind*, is here romanised as Suon Sorin, and *Ghuan Sughambh* as Khuon Sokhamphu.

For a comprehensive history of the Sangkum Reastr Niyum, see: David Chandler, *The Tragedy of Cambodian History: Politics, War, and Revolution Since 1945* (Chiang Mai: Silkworm Books, 1999 [1991]), esp. pp. 85–191. For a Marxist-influenced Khmer critique of the regime, see: Diep Sophal, *Rabab Sangkum Reastr Niyum (1955–1970) Mahā Jay Jamnah Ning Vipatti* [Sangkum Reastr Niyum Regime (1955–1970): Great Victory

was a period of intensified modernisation in almost all sectors of Cambodian society, including industry, education, and urbanisation. Arts and culture were instrumentalised by Sihanouk and his regime as key to the articulation of a new sense of Khmer modernity, and to communicating the achievements of the regime.[2] During its first decade—when Sorin's novel was written—the Sangkum was also defined by its "neutralist" or non-aligned position in the Cold War, which was important as fighting intensified in the Second Indochina War.

The bestselling novel of the Sangkum period, and the inaugural recipient of a prestigious government-sponsored prize,[3] Sorin's is a propagandistic and nationalist endorsement of Sihanouk's modernising regime—yet also a sharp indictment of social inequalities from the years immediately prior to national independence, which continued under the post-independence Sangkum. This tension between celebration and critique is central to the novel's value. *A New Sun Rises Over the Old Land* remains widely read in Cambodia today, and is still prescribed reading in many Cambodian schools and universities. Given its canonical status in the vernacular context, it is fitting that it is now one of the first modern Khmer novels to appear in English translation.[4] Although its narrative and prose may in parts seem quaint or awkward to today's reader,

---

and Crisis], 2nd edn. (Phnom Penh: Jauk Jey, 2009). I use "postcolonial" to refer to the period after national independence from French colonial rule, while also recognising that many continuing forms of coloniality continued after independence, and endure.

[2] See: Ingrid Muan, "Citing Angkor: The 'Cambodian Arts' in the Age of Restoration 1918–2000," unpublished PhD dissertation, Columbia University, New York, 2001, esp. pp. 255–385. See also: Ly Daravuth and Ingrid Muan, eds., *Cultures of Independence: An Introduction to Cambodian Arts and Culture in the 1950's and 1960's* (Phnom Penh: Reyum, 2001). See also: Roger Nelson, "Modernity and Contemporaneity in 'Cambodian Arts' After Independence," unpublished PhD thesis, University of Melbourne, 2017.

[3] Klairung Amratisha, "The Cambodian Novel: A Study of its Emergence and Development," unpublished PhD thesis, School of Oriental and African Studies, University of London, 1998, pp. 214–215.

[4] What very little Khmer literature is available in English translation chiefly consists of folk tales, pre-modern epics, as well as excerpts and short stories. See: David Chandler, *Two Friends Who Tried to Empty the Sea: Eleven Cambodian Folktales* (Melbourne: Monash University Centre for South East Asian Studies Working Paper 8, 1976). See also: George Chigas, *Tum Teav: A Translation and Analysis of a Cambodian Literary Classic* (Phnom Penh: Documentation Center of Cambodia, 2005). See also: Frank Stewart and Sharon May, eds., *In the Shadow of Angkor: Contemporary Writing from Cambodia* (Honolulu: University of Hawaiʻi Press, 2004). See also several bilingual anthologies compiled by Teri Shaffer Yamada, such as: Teri Shaffer Yamada and Soeun Klo, eds., *Gráp Yāng Doembī Anak*

the novel's historical value is great: for the study of society and politics in this period, and also as a resource for art historians, urban researchers, and others. It is hoped that this Cambodian literary response to late colonial and early postcolonial modernisation may be productively compared with fictional works from elsewhere in the region, and beyond. For scholars of nationalism, including those opposed to its insidious effects, it is necessary to study the phenomenon in its many and varied vernacular forms.

Several important and approximately contemporaneous novels and novellas from elsewhere in the region have appeared in English translation, which also depict Southeast Asian characters and their societies during a period of sharp transformation, and derive much of their dramatic tension from resulting conflicts of divergent sensibilities. For example, Vu Trong Phung's *Dumb Luck* was first published in Vietnamese in 1936, and is a satirical portrayal of new fashions and affectations among Hanoi society of its time. *Behind the Painting* by Siburapha (the pen name of Kulāp Sāipradit) was first published in Thai in 1937, and is an emotionally complex study of a Thai man studying and working in Japan. Ma Ma Lay's *Not Out of Hate* was first published in Burmese in 1955, but is also set in the 1930s, and chronicles a clash of worldviews between a young Burmese woman and her wealthy, Anglophile Burmese neighbour. Each of these literary works display key qualities shared by Sorin's

---

Nā: Kamrang Snādai Aksārsilp Khmaer Paep Damnoeb / Who's It For: Collection of Modern Cambodian Short Fiction (Phnom Penh: Nou Hach Literary Association, 2014).

Recently, some short excerpts of Khmer literature from the period before 1975, approximately contemporaneous with Suon Sorin's novel, have appeared. See: Siti Keo, "Crazy for Wandering: Fiction by Kham Pun Kimny," *Words Without Borders,* November 2015. https://www.wordswithoutborders.org/article/crazy-itinerant-walker [Accessed 15 September 2018]. The short article includes translations of a brief letter by Kumny from 1971, and of a work of fiction from 1969. See also: Soth Polin, "The Anarchist," trans. Penny Edwards, *Mekong Review* 1 (November 2015), https://mekongreview.com/the-anarchist/ [Accessed 15 September 2018]. Edwards' translated excerpt is from the French.

There is also a body of work on Khmer literature in French, including translations. Again, the primary focus has not been on modern novels. See, for example: Solange Thierry, *De La Rizière à la Forêt: Contes Khmers* [From the Rice Field to the Forest: Khmer Tales] (Paris: Editions l'Harmattan, 1988). For an example of a modern novel, approximately contemporaneous with Sorin's, translated to French, see: Khun Srun, *L'Accusé* [The Accused], trans. Christophe Macquet (Paris: Les Éditions du Sonneur, 2018). Macquet has also translated short stories from this period to French. See: Soth Polin, *Génial et Génital,* trans. Christophe Macquet (Paris: Le Grand Os, 2017).

A New Sun Rises Over the Old Land, suggesting that throughout the region, many early vernacular novels followed broadly similar literary trends.

Several questions arise when approaching the novel. How do the novel's plot and themes relate to its historical, literary and political contexts? How can this work of literature be understood in mutually illuminating relationship to contemporaneous works of modern "Cambodian art" in other media, such as paintings? How might reading Suon Sorin be valuable for students of the region more broadly? In this short introductory essay, I attempt to address such questions.[5]

Like many modern Khmer novels, Sorin's is a dramatisation of the meeting of opposing worlds: urban and rural, agrarian and proletarian, capitalist aggressors and oppressed precariat, the colonial and the independent.[6]

A New Sun Rises Over the Old Land is the story of Suon Sam, a man in his twenties, born to a "family line of pitiful farmers," who around the early 1950s moves from the province of Battambang to Phnom Penh, in search of opportunity and due to political unrest caused by the Khmer Issarak pro-independence rebels.[7] Sam's life in the city is a series of hardships, and he is soon forced to earn a meagre and precarious living by working as the driver of a rented *cyclo,* or pedalled rickshaw. He is "the very poorest of the poor", and often goes hungry. Sam marries a woman named Soy, who is of a similarly modest socioeconomic position. Aged seventeen, Soy embodies many virtues typically desired in a Cambodian woman: she is "beautiful", "well-liked", "quiet" and "honest with her husband". Necessity requires her to take up paid employment in the home of a wealthy "capitalist" (*nāydun*). Immediately upon arrival in his house, Soy is brutally raped by her employer. Sorin's narration of the event is an indictment of the immorality of the capitalist class, but also functions as a cautionary indication of the perils that await women who stray too far from a domestic environment. Sam is subsequently imprisoned for his attempt to avenge this violent attack. Even during his spell in prison, Sam

---

[5] I will first summarise the novel's narrative in order to point to some important structural elements that Sorin deploys. Readers wishing to preserve the story's surprise may wish to skip ahead to the essay's next section.

[6] The notion of literary structuring around order and disorder draws on David Chandler, "Songs at the Edge of the Forest: Perceptions of Order in Three Cambodian Texts," in *At the Edge of the Forest: Essays on Cambodia, History, and Narrative in Honor of David Chandler,* ed. Anne Ruth Hansen and Judy Ledgerwood (Ithaca, NY: Cornell Southeast Asia Program, 2008), pp. 31–46. The essay was originally written in 1978.

[7] On Khmer Issaraks, see: Chandler, *Tragedy,* esp. pp. 28–57.

encounters an oppressive hierarchy in which he perceives wealth and power to be linked to a Chinese, Vietnamese, or other non-Khmer "ethnicity".

Soy and Sam live in an inner-city community of impoverished workers, including other *cyclo* drivers: "workers who live hand to mouth, working in the morning in order to eat in the evening". Their poverty is in sharp contrast to the opulent life of Phnom Penh's wealthy elite. This focus on inequality, as well as on evictions and other experiences of urban precarity, resonate with Cambodia today, as do many other recurrent concerns in the novel. When Soy falls ill, a doctor refuses to treat her because Sam cannot pay the hefty medical fee, and Soy dies as a result. After this tragedy, Sam returns to driving a *cyclo,* and his life continues as one trial after another. He is tricked and manipulated by "deceitful politicians", imprisoned again for a time, and he suffers repeated crises, both economic and existential. Eventually, a change in employment lifts his prospects, and Sam at last enjoys "a lofty and honoured position" and has the chance to live "prosperously and well" in Phnom Penh as the housekeeper for a young and kindly government employee. The author pithily observes that "living in the city these past few years, Sam's life had been gradually devastated".

Sam's improvement in circumstances is explicitly tied to that of the nation, heralded by independence from colonial rule—an achievement which is generally credited to Sihanouk's "crusade for independence". Sorin triumphantly declares that "all classes of the Khmer people, both in the city and in the countryside, had also received tranquillity and happiness, without fear of further insecurity". Despite this, Sam returns to Battambang and resumes life as a farmer, following Sihanouk's call: "His Royal Highness the Father of National Independence had royally decreed to his fellow compatriots that they must remember our rice fields, for those rice fields are the basis and foundation of the national economy." Closely conforming to historical events, this incident refers to Sihanouk's rhetorical policy of "Khmer Buddhist Socialism", which was in reality little more than a new way of articulating the longstanding economic and social reliance on rice agriculture.[8]

The protagonist's decision to leave his comfortable new job in Phnom Penh and return to farming might be read in at least four ways. It may be a

---

[8] For a discussion of Khmer Buddhist Socialism in relation to modern painting of the period, see: Roger Nelson, "'The Work the Nation Depends On': Landscapes and Women in the Paintings of Nhek Dim," in *Ambitious Alignments: New Histories of Southeast Asian Art,* ed. Stephen H. Whiteman, Sarena Abdullah, Yvonne Low, Phoebe Scott, (Sydney and Singapore: Power Publications and National Gallery Singapore, 2018), pp. 19–48.

sign of Sam's devotion to Sihanouk, and willingness to follow his directives. It may also be a sign of Sihanouk's success in eliminating the political insecurity caused by the Khmer Issarak rebels, which had been an important factor driving Sam's relocation from Battambang in the first place. Or it may be a far-fetched narrative turn, that diminishes the plausibility of Sorin's characterisation of Sam. Perhaps it is a sign that Sam's life in the city, although improved, was still far from ideal.

This entire narrative is recounted as a kind of flashback that Sam experiences while riding the train from Battambang to Phnom Penh. He is travelling in order to attend a National Congress: a regularly occurring event during the Sangkum Reastr Niyum period, at which Sihanouk's rule and his closeness to his citizen-subjects was performed as public spectacle. The novel opens with a scene of Sam on the train, musing on his past, which constitutes the bulk of the action. Its concluding chapters consist of Sam—whose train has arrived in the city—describing life in Phnom Penh under the new regime. He marvels at the electrification of the capital, the appearance of grand new buildings and monuments, and the general modernisation of life and of the urban environment.

The contrast between these celebratory final chapters of the novel, and the preceding descriptions of injustice and hardship, serve two seemingly contradictory yet also related functions. On the one hand, the propagandistic image of joy, comfort and security under the postcolonial Sangkum Reastr Niyum regime is emphasised through its sharp contrast with the suffering of life during the final years of French colonial control. This narrative of an immediate transformation in circumstances following national independence perpetuates a Sihanouk-sponsored myth, unsubstantiated by historical evidence. Yet on the other hand, the temporal ambiguity in the narrative—heightened by the extended flashback structure—raises the possibility that inequality and impoverishment continue even under Sihanouk's rule. The Prince himself is irreproachable, in the novel as in all public discourse during the period. Yet the postcolonial society had its flaws, and like many other Khmer novelists of the period, Sorin was unflinching in his depiction of these.[9] The social and economic inequality that the novel's characters embody continued under the new regime, as did the precariousness of life for the urban poor, and the cruel disdain which the wealthy elite felt for them.

---

[9] For more on "social novels", which centred on critiques of Sangkum Reastr Niyum-era life, see: Amratisha, "Cambodian Novel," pp. 241–250.

On approaching Khmer literature

My desire to situate *A New Sun Rises Over the Old Land* in its social and historical context is informed in part by a critical-pedagogical curriculum text, written in Khmer in 1963 by a professor of literature named Khuon Sokhamphu. In it, the author asks, "What is it that we call literature?" He suggests that literature is "words that are the voice of our inner emotions". It is "a kind of knowledge that shares discussions through letters, using an artfulness [*tôy silpvithī*] to make it sound lovely and interesting for the reader". With this in mind, the curriculum continues, "in order to make our study of literature useful, we must study literature in connection to civilisation. That is, whatever we study about literature, we will study about people."[10]

There are three significant points to observe in this passage. First, literature is "a kind of knowledge that shares discussions": that is, Sokhamphu situates the literary in an active relationship to other forms of discourse, other kinds of knowledge and other discussions. Knowledge is implicitly understood as being constituted in networks that intersect. Second, the author emphasises the importance of the specifically aesthetic qualities of literature: its "artfulness" that is "lovely and interesting". The formal qualities of writing are valued, and worthy of study. And third, the passage positions "the reader" as central to the understanding of literature.

Sokhamphu's curriculum has long since fallen into obscurity, and does not seem to have been cited in any previous studies of modern Khmer literature in Khmer, English, or French.[11] But here I try to heed his suggestions, especially for the study of literature in relation to culture and society.

This is not to deny that Sokhamphu's words echo those of numerous other scholars in the region and beyond. And although this text is written in Khmer, Sokhamphu received his doctoral degree from Humboldt University in Berlin, and also circulated in both Anglophone and Francophone settings during the 1960s and 1970s, including publishing an essay in a regionally influential

---

[10] Khuon Sokhamphu, *Lamnām Siksā Aksarsāstra Khmaer* [Course for Study of Khmer Literature] (Phnom Penh: National Pedagogical Institute, 1963), pp. 1–6. National Archives of Cambodia, Phnom Penh, Box B-186.

[11] For more on Sokhamphu, see: Khing Hoc Dy, ed., *Gamrang Ātthabad Khemara Siksā Yuddis Jūn Bandit Sabhācāry Khin Sok, Sāstrācāry Khuon Sokhamphu, Bandit Sabhācāry Long Seam* [Selected Documents in Khmer Studies, in Honour of Professors Khin Sok, Khuon Sokhamphu, and Long Seam] (Phnom Penh: Editions Angkor, 2013), esp. pp. 19–21.

scholarly journal which is still cited by linguists today.[12] Yet I foreground Sokhamphu here in an effort to situate my approach in a local discourse, and specifically in Khmer. As a gesture toward de-imperialising theory, this is of course insufficient. But as an attempt to understand the network of discourses in the Cambodian and especially the Khmer setting during this period, perhaps it may be of some modest use.

Several other Khmer-language studies of Khmer literature share Sokhamphu's emphasis on the centrality of sociocultural contexts to interpreting novels. Im Proum notes that "difficulties in people's lives in their society" is a predominant theme in modern fiction.[13] In another example, Khing Hoc Dy divides twentieth-century Khmer literature into six periods, which correspond precisely to shifting political regimes. Moreover, he explicitly links the "strong progress" of literature in the Sangkum Reastr Niyum period—during which Sorin's novel was published—to infrastructural changes of the time, specifically the establishment of universities.[14] A textbook published around 2012 (and commonly used by secondary school teachers in Phnom Penh at the time of writing in 2018) also emphasises ways in which Sorin's novel relates to historical events of its period. "An important point that the author raises is about the hardships suffered by poor people", the textbook notes of Sorin's novel. It also makes special mention that "in this novel, the author describes events from the history of the Sangkum Reastr Niyum".[15]

Of course, close analysis of the novel's text itself is also necessary and important, and interpretation based solely on the novel's various contexts will overlook the literary and other qualities of Sorin's writing. Here, I have chosen to focus chiefly on elements outside of the text, relating to the author, the novel's reading publics, the functions of Khmer literature, and its relationship to other forms of modern art in Cambodia, especially modern painting. It

---

[12] Khuon Sokhamphu, "The Case of Diversity in Cambodian Dialects," *Journal of the Siam Society* 63, No. 2 (1975): 78–85.

[13] Im Proum, "Modern Novel," in Franklin E. Huffman and Im Proum, *Cambodian Literary Reader and Glossary* (New Haven and London: Yale University Press, 1977), p. 19. In Khmer.

[14] Khing Hoc Dy, *Aksarsilp Khmaer Satavatsa Dī 20 Kavinibandh Ning Kamrang Atthabad* [Khmer Literature of the 20th Century: Authors and Texts] (Phnom Penh: Editions Angkor, 2007), pp. 33–34.

[15] These quotations are from a textbook titled *Siav Bhau Grū Aksarsāstra Khmaer 12* [Teacher's Book: Khmer Literature 12], published by the Ministry of Education, Youth and Sports, around 2012. The book was kindly shared with me by Chin Setha, in personal communications, July 2018.

is my hope that this may provide a foundation for other studies in future, which may more closely attend to the text itself, since it is now available to an Anglophone readership.

Of particular interest for future research on this text may be the author's use of character names with ironic or other connotations, and also the recurrent focus on criticisms of society at Sorin's time of writing which continue to resonate today. The principal characters' names are all short, and connote "Khmerness" which distinguishes them from many other incidental figures, whose names connote Chinese or other mixed heritage. Some incidental characters' names, as well as some place names referred to in the text, further connote wealth or other virtues, often seemingly at odds with the hardships that Sam and Soy experience. Some key examples of these are indicated in footnotes, as are some key instances of actual places which are referred to in the text. Some aspects of society repeatedly criticised in the novel which may resonate with Cambodia today include economic and other forms of inequality, traffic, insufficient healthcare, and housing precarity caused by evictions. Also significant is the novel's recurrent fixation on race and ethnicity. The "capitalists" and wealthy figures in the novel are all given names which connote Chinese heritage, and Sam—and by implication Sorin—is often mistrustful of Chinese Khmers. Other characters at times voice other perceptions of ethnic differences, such as the belief that Chinese and Vietnamese workers are more productive or diligent than their Khmer counterparts. These and other elements within the novel's text itself will reward further study.

On Suon Sorin, and "dark, black clouds"

Suon Sorin was born on 9 July 1930, in the Sangker district of Battambang, Cambodia. *A New Sun Rises Over the Old Land* is his only known work of fiction. He joined the Association of Khmer Writers on 13 June 1961. He was also employed as the Secretary of the Battambang Provincial Administration Office.[16] Twelve years earlier in 1949, while a monk in Phnom Penh's Wat Langka pagoda and around nineteen years old, Sorin published an account in the influential Khmer journal *Kambujasuriya* of the funeral of a Pali teacher at

---

[16] This biographical information is from Khing Hoc Dy, *Aksarsilp Khmaer Satavatsa Dī 20*, p. 285. In personal communications, in July 2017, Professor Hoc Dy—preeminent expert on modern Khmer literature—confirmed that this is derived from his research notes, made in 1970, and that no additional information is known.

the Wat Po Veal pagoda.[17] Also appearing in the same issue of *Kambujasuriya* is the novelist Nhok Them (1903–1974), author of one of Cambodia's earliest modern novels, *The Rose of Pailin* (*Kulāb Pailin*, published 1943). This suggests that Sorin was familiar with Khmer modern literature such as this, and perhaps also had some interaction with the generation of novelists who preceded him.

Very little else is known of the author of *A New Sun Rises Over the Old Land*. His personal papers have been lost, the circumstances of his death are unclear, and no surviving family has been located.

Despite the prominence and unparalleled popularity of his novel, this uncertainty around Suon Sorin's biography is a common circumstance when researching arts and culture in Cambodia from this period—a time which is now described not only as postcolonial, but also as pre-war. Between 1975 and 1979, Pot Pot's radical agrarian communist regime, commonly known as the Khmer Rouge, ruled Cambodia. An estimated 1.7 million Cambodians perished during these years, approximating nearly a quarter of the nation's population at the time; this tragedy is usually described as a genocide. It is widely believed that between 80 and 90 per cent of all artists and intellectuals died during these years, often deliberately targeted as representatives of pre-revolutionary culture. Numerous books, archival records, and artworks were also either destroyed or dispersed.[18]

---

[17] This article is published across three issues of *Kambujasuriya* during 1949: No. 4, pp. 312–317; No. 5, pp. 386–394 and No. 6, pp. 470–477. Copies of the journal are held in the archives of the Buddhist Institute in Phnom Penh. They are also reproduced at http://khmerword.blogspot.sg/2012/07/blog-post_2077.html [Accessed November 2017]. Although it is not certain that the author of this article was the same Suon Sorin who wrote the novel, Khing Hoc Dy believes that this is likely. As Hoc Dy observes, officially recorded dates of birth for Cambodians during this period are often unreliable, so Sorin may have been older than records indicate. Training as a monk would also have equipped him well for his career in the civil service. Khing Hoc Dy, personal communications, July 2017.

On *Kambujasuriya* and its historical significance, see: George Chigas, "The Emergence of Twentieth Century Literary Institutions: the Case of Kambujasuriya," in *The Canon in Southeast Asian Literatures: Literatures of Burma, Cambodia, Indonesia, Laos, Malaysia, the Philippines, Thailand and Vietnam*, ed. David Smyth (Richmond, UK: Curzon, 2000), pp. 135–146.

[18] The claim first appears in writing in: Chheng Phon, "Mati Tamnāng Silpakar" [Views of a Representative of Artists], in *Ūkritdhakamm Rabás Panavādi Anuttarabhābniyam Cin Pekāng Ning Parivār Pol Pot – Ieng Sary – Khieu Samphan Knung Amlung Chnām 1975–1979* [The Crimes of the Beijing-ist Clique and the Pol Pot – Ieng Sary – Khieu Samphan Stooges 1975–1979] (Phnom Penh: National Advisory Alliance for Solidarity,

Many Cambodians today believe that Suon Sorin was among those to perish under the Khmer Rouge.

Any effort to historicise *A New Sun Rises Over the Old Land*—to situate it in the optimistic postcolonial moment in which it was written—must always also take into account the Khmer Rouge atrocities which followed so soon thereafter. The artist and scholar Chheng Phon (1930–2016) described the legacy of the Khmer Rouge as a "heavy rock [that] will weigh down on us for many hundreds of years to come".[19] With the benefit of hindsight, we may discern a haunting prescience in Sihanouk's words, quoted in the penultimate chapter of Sorin's novel. Addressing the Ninth National Congress in 1960, and using imagery which recalls that in the novel's title, the Prince and former King warned ominously:

> on the future horizon of our country, there are dark, black clouds; they make us worry that we will not have enough peace to build our nation and continue to grow, progress and move forward.

The shadow cast by the Khmer Rouge over all subsequent research and creative endeavour in Cambodia is inescapable. The novelist Soth Polin (1943–), a contemporary of Sorin's who has published in Khmer as well as in French, describes the experience:

> There is something that we cannot get past. It just kills the imagination. It is the atrocity of the Khmer Rouge. Even if you are reaching in your imagination for a new destination, you cannot get past their cruelty. When you try to write something without mentioning the Khmer Rouge, you can't. The next generation will forgive that, they will forget, but for us, we cannot forgive it.[20]

Construction and Defence of the Motherland, 1983), pp. 50–57. National Archives of Cambodia, Phnom Penh, Box B-637. As well as being an artist and scholar, Chheng Phon was the Minister of Culture after 1979, responsible for gathering artists who had survived the preceding years, and overseeing the "rebuilding" of the arts. By 1988, the figure of 80 to 90 per cent of artists having died had appeared in a scholarly setting in English: Sam Sam-Ang, "The *Pin Peat* Ensemble: Its History, Music, and Context," unpublished PhD dissertation, Wesleyan University, Connecticut, 1988, pp. 282–283.

[19] Chheng Phon, "Views of a Representative of Artists," p. 55.

[20] Soth Polin had been taught French poetry by Saloth Sar (who later took the name Pol Pot), at a private school in Phnom Penh in 1957. Sharon May, "Beyond Words: An Interview with Soth Polin," in *In the Shadow of Angkor: Contemporary Writing from Cambodia,* ed. Frank Stewart and Sharon May (Honolulu: University of Hawai'i Press, 2004), pp. 16–17.

A key historical value in *A New Sun Rises Over the Old Land* is its insight into the nature of nationalist thought during the first decade of Sihanouk's Sangkum Reastr Niyum regime. It is notable that many of the novel's most conspicuous nationalist tropes, such as its idealisation of the Cambodian countryside and its wariness toward urban life and toward Chinese and Vietnamese people, were also taken up in remarkably similar form by Pol Pot's Khmer Rouge in the following decade.

On the novel's reception, and the instrumentalisation of literature

A New Sun Rises Over the Old Land was the inaugural winner of the Indradevi Literary Competition, a prize established by Sihanouk in 1961, soon after founding the Association of Khmer Writers. Sorin's success would certainly have been prominently celebrated. After all, as Klairung Amratisha explains, the Association was supported by Sihanouk "politically, socially and financially". The Prince served as its honorary president, many senior members also held important government positions, and the prize ceremony was funded by the Palace.[21]

Yet beyond this official recognition, it is impossible to judge the reading public's reception of the novel at the time of its publication, because Sihanouk closely controlled the press, and no critical reviews of the novel were published.[22] Anecdotal evidence gathered in recent years suggests that it is widely enjoyed by new generations of readers, more than many other novels published at the time, or in the decades since. Numerous short stories published in the twenty-first century have directly referred to Sorin's novel, either in their titles, or through their focus on *cyclo* drivers as protagonists.[23] This demonstrates its continuing appeal.

---

[21] Amratisha, "Cambodian Novel," pp. 173–174.

[22] On Sihanouk's control of the press, see Chandler, *Tragedy,* pp. 123–124.

[23] See, for example, Phou Chakriya, "Thngai Min Rah" [The Sun Never Rises], in *Gráp Yāng Doembī Anak Nā: Kamrang Snādai Aksārsilp Khmaer Paep Damnoeb / Who's It For: Collection of Modern Cambodian Short Fiction,* ed. Teri Shaffer Yamada and Soeun Klo (Phnom Penh: Nou Hach Literary Association, 2014), pp. 66–80. In Khmer and English, with translation by NH Translation Group. Her story is also the tale of a *cyclo* driver. See also Som Sophearin, *Bel Thngai Rah* [When the Sun Rises] (Phnom Penh: Angkor Thom, 2008). Sophearin's novel centres on the lives of peasants. In 2017, the 21-year-old writer Bun Theanchhay won the Kampot Readers and Writers Festival's Cambodian Emerging Writers competition with a story about a *cyclo* driver, titled "Hands Will Always Have

Sihanouk's establishment of the Indradevi Literary Competition was an act in keeping with many other Southeast Asian regimes at the time. In Burma, for example, the newly installed military government in 1964 established several national literary prizes. One scholar of Burmese literature has claimed that in the decades since, "increasingly, political rather than literary criteria have come to determine the choice of prize-winners".[24] In a linking of specific partisan political allegiance with vague nationalist sentiment, closely recalling Sihanouk's statements, Burmese works were required to support the ruling party, while also "foster[ing] Burmese culture and the Burmese way of life".[25]

In a speech given at the ceremony when awarding Sorin his prize, Sihanouk asserted that writers had a responsibility not only to literature, but also to nation-building. He insisted that writers were duty-bound to support the Sangkum Reastr Niyum government's policy, yet that novels should not write directly about politics.[26]

This is probably the most explicit directive that Sihanouk delivered about the role of culture in this period, and thus likely had much broader implications for "Cambodian artists", beyond the realm of literature. The Prince took a strong and active interest in the arts. He described himself as an artist (indeed, as having been "born an artist"[27]), and he directed numerous movies, including nine documentaries and twelve fiction films between 1960

Fingers." See Daphne Chen, "Traditional, Modern Very Much on the Mind at Kampot Literary Fest," *The Phnom Penh Post,* 6 November 2017. Available online at: http://www. phnompenhpost.com/lifestyle/traditional-modern-very-much-mind-kampot-literary-fest [Accessed November 2017].

[24] Anna Allott, "Introduction" in Ma Ma Lay, *Not Out of Hate: A Novel of Burma,* trans. Margaret Aung-Thwin, ed. William H. Frederick (Athens, Ohio: Ohio University Center for International Studies, 1991), p. xiii.

[25] Anna Allott, "Continuity and Change in the Burmese Literary Canon," in *The Canon in Southeast Asian Literatures: Literatures of Burma, Cambodia, Indonesia, Laos, Malaysia, the Philippines, Thailand and Vietnam,* ed. David Smyth (Richmond, UK: Curzon, 2000), pp. 29–30. Literary prizes were established earlier in Laos, with four contests held under French rule, between 1941 and 1945. See: Chairat Polmuk, "Invoking the Past: The Cultural Politics of Lao Literature, 1941–1975," Master of Arts thesis, Cornell University, Ithaca, NY, 2014, p. 16.

[26] Amratisha, "Cambodian Novel," p. 174.

[27] Sihanouk told a journalist in 1973 that "I am an artist. I was born an artist and what I like best is the cinema, music, literature…". Quoted in Gerard Brissé, "Introduction," in Norodom Sihanouk, *War and Hope: The Case for Cambodia,* trans. Mary Feeney (New York: Pantheon, 1980), p. xxiii.

and 1970 alone.[28] He was photographed painting at an easel within the palace, and he was also a collector of paintings and patron of the visual arts.[29] Yet it seems that in no field aside from literature did Sihanouk make such firm and prescriptive statements about what art should do in order to serve the new nation. In his own films, and in his patronage of painters, musicians, and others, Sihanouk was also making clear statements about the kind of art that he deemed appropriate, and the impossibility of political criticality within it. Yet it was seemingly only in relation to Khmer literature that Sihanouk issued such a direct instruction; in his other activities, and in relation to other art forms, his views on the role of culture were instead heavily implied, but not explicitly prescribed. Literature's rhetorical power seems to have made it especially ripe for political instrumentalisation.

Yet the tension between celebration and critique, especially evident in *A New Sun Rises Over the Old Land,* means that despite being instrumentalised by Sihanouk, the novel resists being rendered simply subservient to the regime. Sorin champions the Sangkum Reastr Niyum regime and its policies, while also sharply decrying the injustices and difficulties of life during the period. The novel demonstrates the value of close readings of works of art and literature, even those which appear to function as "propaganda".

On the *cyclo*, the "Cambodian arts", and the city

Sorin's was among the first Khmer novels to centre on the character of a *cyclo* driver, and seems to have served as a model for numerous others published in the succeeding decade. These subsequent novels also positioned *cyclo* drivers as emblematic of social and economic inequality and precarity. In one novel by Kim Set, published around the same time as Sorin's, the protagonist desperately hopes that his "little hut" can be improved, meanwhile noting that "the owner of his *cyclo* [from whom he rented it] had built a new seven-storey house, built on the sweat of the poor".[30]

---

[28] Eliza Romey, "King, Politician, Artist: The Films of Norodom Sihanouk," unpublished Master of Arts thesis, La Trobe University, Melbourne, 1998, p. 19.

[29] As a collector and patron, Sihanouk had a particular liking for Nhek Dim (1934–1978), a painter famous for his depictions of the Cambodian landscape, who also painted a scene of a *cyclo* riding past the Independence Monument, which is discussed below.

[30] Kim Set (*Gym Saet*), *Dyk Hŭr Min Ceh Hát* [The Water Flows Tirelessly] (Phnom Penh: Srei Bunchon, 2003 [c. 1960s]), p. 5.

Nhek Dim. Title Unknown. Ca. 1960s. Medium, dimensions and location unknown. Image from: Lors Chinda, *Nhek Dim* (Phnom Penh: Lors Chinda Art Publishers, 2001). Reproduced with kind permission of Mr Vandy Dim Nhek.

This focus on drivers was commonly found in literature and cinema throughout the region. In the Khmer setting, an early example is *Sim Anak Bar Lān* [Sim the Chauffeur] by Im Thok, a 1956 novel about a chauffeur who drives a car for a wealthy family.[31] Perhaps the best-known novel in English translation about a transport worker is Lao She's *Rickshaw Boy*, first published in Chinese in the 1930s.[32] The similarities in Lao She's description of his protagonist, Xiangzi, are striking, especially the visceral emphasis on the sweat and physical hardship of pulling the rickshaw. In 1955, a Malay-language film centred on a pedicab driver was one of the first wave of Malay-directed feature films, and enjoyed great success in Singapore and Malaya.[33] In

---

[31] Im Thok, *Sim Anak Bar Lān* [Sim the Chauffeur] (Phnom Penh: Editions Angkor, 2007).

[32] Lao She, *Rickshaw Boy*, trans. Howard Goldblatt (London: Harper Collins, 2010 [1936–37]). The novel's title has also been translated as *Camel Xiangzi*. It is possible that Sorin may have seen the novel, which first appeared in English translation in 1945, however this is unlikely. It is also unlikely that Sorin would have read English.

[33] P. Ramlee, director, *Penarek Bechar*, produced by Malay Film Productions, distributed by Shaw Brothers. The film was discussed at the lecture "Hang Tuah in a Time of

Pann Tra. *Cyclo*. 1960. Medium, dimensions, and location unknown. Image from *Free World*, 1961. Reproduced with kind permission of Mr Vuth Lyno.

Vietnamese, Nguyen Cong Hoan's *Man-Horse, Horse-Man* (*Người Ngựa Ngựa Người*), published in the early 1930s, is also about a rickshaw driver.[34] More recently, the acclaimed Vietnamese film *Cyclo,* released in 1995, depicts the challenges of proletarian life in Ho Chi Minh City.[35] Other examples may be found across the region.

While similar to rickshaws and pedicabs found elsewhere, the *cyclo* was in fact invented in Phnom Penh in 1937, by French engineer Maurice Coupeaud. It was subsequently exported to Saigon and elsewhere: Coupeaud himself pedalled a *cyclopousse* (as they are formally known in French) all the way from Phnom Penh to Saigon, in a dramatic and effective publicity stunt.[36] It rapidly became a ubiquitous form of transport in Phnom Penh, its popularity only eclipsed in the 2000s with an increased number of motorcycles and motorised tuk-tuks.

The invention of the *cyclo* notably coincides with the emergence of Khmer modern novels, as well as modern representational painting techniques. The prominence of *cyclo* in Khmer novels, and also in paintings made during the Sangkum Reastr Niyum period, may be understood not only as a means to discuss socioeconomic inequality and precarity, but also as a representative symbol of all that was new in the modernising city. Driving a *cyclo* was a historically recent form of employment, and riding one was a novel form of transport.

Only a small handful of paintings made by Cambodians before 1975 that depict the modern city are known to survive; the vast majority of the few hundred extant paintings from this period are of rural environments.[37] Archival records indicate that many other artists also painted the new buildings of the modern city during the early 1960s, but these images all appear to have been lost. Thus, the very few known surviving paintings from before 1975 that depict the modern city take on a special significance for art historians.

Independence: Malay Texts in the 1950s and 1960s," delivered by Timothy P. Barnard at the National Library Singapore on 21 October 2017, to coincide with the exhibition *Tales of the Malay World: Manuscripts and Early Books.*

[34] I am grateful to Dương Mạnh Hùng for bringing this novel to my attention. It has not yet been translated to English.

[35] Tran Anh Hung, director, *Xích Lô (Cyclo),* produced by Christophe Rossignon, distributed by New Yorker Video and Gaumont.

[36] Milton Osborne, *Phnom Penh: A Cultural History* (Oxford and New York: Oxford University Press, 2008), p. 91.

[37] On 20th-century painting in Cambodia, see: Muan, "Citing Angkor." See also: Nelson, "Modernity and Contemporaneity in 'Cambodian Arts'."

Two surviving paintings of Phnom Penh, contemporaneous with Sorin's novel, depict a *cyclo* in motion. One is by Nhek Dim (1934–1978), the most popular painter of the time, who was closely associated with the United States Information Service, and with Sihanouk.[38] The other painting is by Pann Tra (1931–2009), an artist who was a senior member of a communist-affiliated painters' association, independent from and critical of Sihanouk.[39] Given that no written sources relating to these paintings have been found—and writings on visual art in Cambodia were scant at that time—novels about *cyclo* drivers, such as *A New Sun Rises Over the Old Land*, provide valuable contextual information which is crucial for understanding these art-historically significant images.

These images may also prove illuminating for our understanding of this novel, and in particular its relationship to the city, and to the multi-layered sense of temporality that inheres in the Cambodian modern.

In both paintings, the *cyclo* driver's strenuous physical effort is emphasised. In Nhek Dim's work, the driver is hunched, cowering under a heavy rainstorm. In Pann Tra's painting, the driver's lean muscles are emphasised. The simultaneously pitiable and admirable figure of the *cyclo* driver, and his specifically masculine vitality, may be seen in these images—as in this novel— to function like a symbol for that of the new nation.[40]

In both paintings, also as in the novel, the novel form of transport that is the *cyclo* is linked to the recent transformations in the urban environment. In Pann Tra's work, the repeated parallel lines of the vehicle are echoed by the electric powerlines visible in the background. This compositional device draws the viewer's attention to the historically recent electrification of the Cambodian capital—a phenomenon also described in wondrous terms in Sorin's novel, as Sam describes "electric lights burning as bright as day [...] Along every street, and in all the big shops and cinemas, there were electric lights in red, blue and yellow, that enchanted the eye". In Nhek Dim's painting, the *cyclo* travels past a fountain and the Independence Monument, both erected in the late 1950s to celebrate the nation's independence from colonial rule. While the artist's adherence to linear perspective renders the Independence Monument small

[38] On Nhek Dim, see: Nelson, "'The Work the Nation Depends On'," and Muan, "Citing Angkor," esp. pp. 306–319.
[39] On Pann Tra, see: Pann Tra, "A Conversation with Pen Tra," in *Cultures of Independence: An Introduction to Cambodian Arts and Culture in the 1950's and 1960's*, edited by Ly Daravuth and Ingrid Muan (Phnom Penh: Reyum, 2001), pp. 271–294. Thanks also to personal communications with Pann Tra's grandson, Vuth Lyno, in Phnom Penh from 2012–2017.
[40] See: Simon Creak, *Embodied Nation: Sport, Masculinity and the Making of Modern Laos* (Honolulu: University of Hawai'i Press, 2015).

in his composition, its symbolic significance is nevertheless conveyed by its being bathed in a bright light, as if situated in a spot of sunshine in the eye of the rainstorm that otherwise envelopes the scene.

Prominently sited at a major intersection in the city centre, the landmark Independence Monument and fountain also feature in Sorin's novel. Sam observes: "A beautiful monument had risen in place of the former Koun Kat Bridge, which before had been a foul-smelling place. The monument's fine decorations were no different from those at Angkor Wat. It was a memorial for Independence…." This sense of awe at the dramatically transforming capital—a city in which the Cambodian authorities during the previous century had for several years resisted French colonial attempts to construct buildings in concrete[41]—is shared in paintings, films, pop songs, and novels of the period. One popular psychedelic rock song, titled *Cyclo* and popularised in the early 1970s by singer Yol Aularang,[42] suggests that this mode of transport was seen as chic and modern. The song's lyrics associate riding a *cyclo* with sexual flirtation, in specifically named locations across Phnom Penh.

Sam's observation of the Independence Monument's "fine decorations" being "no different from those at Angkor Wat" is telling. In fact, the ornamentation on the monument is modelled on the tenth-century temple of Banteay Srei, while the tower's overall shape follows that of the central towers at the twelfth-century temple of Angkor Wat. These references to ancient Cambodian Hindu-Buddhist temples are grafted onto the twentieth-century rationalist geometry of Le Corbusier's principles of proportion, which govern the repeated right angles in the monument's support structure.[43]

These architectural details point to the multiple temporalities that are woven together in the making of a modern aesthetic in Cambodia. The modern comprises the Khmer and the cosmopolitan, the new and the ancient, together and at once. This coevality of plural times is at the heart of *A New Sun Rises Over the Old Land*. The novel's very title points to the conjoining of the recent and the ancient. This fine balance, like many other forms of tension within the novel, is a key to its lasting appeal.

---

[41] Penny Edwards, *Cambodge: The Cultivation of a Nation, 1860–1945* (Chiang Mai: Silkworm, 2007), p. 44.

[42] With thanks to Oum Rotanak Oudom of the Cambodia Vintage Music Association, personal communications, 2017.

[43] On the symbolic functions of the Independence Monument, see: Roger Nelson, "Phnom Penh's Independence Monument and Vientiane's Patuxai: Complex Symbols of Postcolonial Nationhood in Cold War-era Southeast Asia," in *Monument Culture: International Perspectives on the Future of Monuments in a Changing World,* ed. Laura Macaluso (Lanham, MD: Rowman & Littlefield, 2019), pp. 35–48.

Bibliography

Allott, Anna. "Introduction." In Ma Ma Lay. *Not Out of Hate: A Novel of Burma*, translated by Margaret Aung-Thwin, edited by William H. Frederick, pp. xii–xxviii. Athens, Ohio: Ohio University Center for International Studies, 1991.

Allott, Anna. "Continuity and Change in the Burmese Literary Canon." In *The Canon in Southeast Asian Literatures: Literatures of Burma, Cambodia, Indonesia, Laos, Malaysia, the Philippines, Thailand and Vietnam*, edited by David Smyth, pp. 21–40. Richmond, UK: Curzon, 2000.

Amratisha, Klairung. "The Cambodian Novel: A Study of its Emergence and Development." PhD thesis. School of Oriental and African Studies, University of London, 1998.

Brissé, Gerard. "Introduction." In Norodom Sihanouk. *War and Hope: The Case for Cambodia*, translated by Mary Feeney, pp. xiii–xl. New York: Pantheon, 1980.

Chandler, David. *Two Friends Who Tried to Empty the Sea: Eleven Cambodian Folktales*. Melbourne: Monash University Centre for South East Asian Studies Working Paper 8, 1976.

Chandler, David. *The Tragedy of Cambodian History: Politics, War, and Revolution Since 1945*. Chiang Mai: Silkworm Books, 1999 [1991].

Chandler, David. "Songs at the Edge of the Forest: Perceptions of Order in Three Cambodian Texts." In *At the Edge of the Forest: Essays on Cambodia, History, and Narrative in Honor of David Chandler*, edited by Anne Ruth Hansen and Judy Ledgerwood, pp. 31–46. Ithaca, NY: Cornell Southeast Asia Program, 2008.

Chen, Daphne. "Traditional, Modern Very Much on the Mind at Kampot Literary Fest." *The Phnom Penh Post,* 6 November 2017. Available online at: http://www.phnompenhpost.com/lifestyle/traditional-modern-very-much-mind-kampot-literary-fest [accessed November 2017].

Chheng Phon. "Mati Tamnāng Silpakar" [Views of a Representative of Artists]. In *Ūkritdhakamm Rabás Panavādi Anuttarabhābniyam Cin Pekāng Ning Parivār Pol Pot – Ieng Sary – Khieu Samphan Knung Amlung Chnām 1975–1979* [The Crimes of the Beijing-ist Clique and the Pol Pot – Ieng Sary – Khieu Samphan Stooges 1975–1979], pp. 50–57. Phnom Penh: National Advisory Alliance for Solidarity, Construction and Defence of the Motherland, 1983. National Archives of Cambodia, Phnom Penh, Box B-637.

Chigas, George. "The Emergence of Twentieth Century Literary Institutions: The Case of Kambujasuriya." In *The Canon in Southeast Asian Literatures: Literatures of Burma, Cambodia, Indonesia, Laos, Malaysia, the Philippines, Thailand and Vietnam*, edited by David Smyth, 135–146. Richmond, UK: Curzon, 2000.

Chigas, George. *Tum Teav: A Translation and Analysis of a Cambodian Literary Classic*. Phnom Penh: Documentation Center of Cambodia, 2005.

Creak, Simon. *Embodied Nation: Sport, Masculinity and the Making of Modern Laos*. Honolulu: University of Hawai'i Press, 2015.

Diep Sophal. *Rabab Sangkum Reastr Niyum (1955–1970) Mahā Jay Jamnah Ning Vipatti* [Sangkum Reastr Niyum Regime (1955–1970): Great Victory and Crisis]. 2nd edition. Phnom Penh: Jauk Jey, 2009.

Edwards, Penny. *Cambodge: The Cultivation of a Nation, 1860–1945*. Chiang Mai: Silkworm, 2007.

Im Proum. "Modern Novel." In Franklin E. Huffman and Im Proum. *Cambodian Literary Reader and Glossary*, p. 19. New Haven and London: Yale University Press, 1977.

Im Thok. *Sim Anak Bar Lān* [Sim the Chauffeur]. Phnom Penh: Editions Angkor, 2007 [1956].

Khing Hoc Dy. *Aksarsilp Khmaer Satavatsa Dī 20 Kavinibandh Ning Kamrang Atthabad* [Khmer Literature of the 20th Century: Authors and Texts]. Phnom Penh: Editions Angkor, 2007.

Khing Hoc Dy, editor. *Gamrang Ātthabad Khemara Siksā Yuddis Jūn Bandit Sabhācāry Khin Sok, Sāstrācāry Khuon Sokhamphu, Bandit Sabhācāry Long Seam* [Selected Documents in Khmer Studies, in Honour of Professors Khin Sok, Khuon Sokhamphu, and Long Seam]. Phnom Penh: Editions Angkor, 2013.

Khuon Sokhamphu. *Lamnām Siksā Aksarsāstra Khmaer* [Course for Study of Khmer Literature], pp. 1–6. Phnom Penh: National Pedagogical Institute, 1963. National Archives of Cambodia, Phnom Penh, Box B-186.

Khuon Sokhamphu. "The Case of Diversity in Cambodian Dialects." *Journal of the Siam Society* 63, No. 2 (1975): 78–85.

Kim Set (*Gym Saet*). *Dyk Hūr Min Ceh Hát* [The Water Flows Tirelessly]. Phnom Penh: Srei Bunchon, 2003 [c. 1960s].

Lao She. *Rickshaw Boy*. Translated by Howard Goldblatt. London: Harper Collins, 2010 [1936–37].

Ly Daravuth and Ingrid Muan, editors. *Cultures of Independence: An Introduction to Cambodian Arts and Culture in the 1950's and 1960's*. Phnom Penh: Reyum, 2001.

Ma Ma Lay. *Not Out of Hate: A Novel of Burma*. Translated by Margaret Aung-Thwin, edited by William H. Frederick. Athens, Ohio: Ohio University Center for International Studies, 1991.

May, Sharon. "Beyond Words: An Interview with Soth Polin." In *In the Shadow of Angkor: Contemporary Writing from Cambodia*, edited by Frank Stewart and Sharon May, pp. 9–20. Honolulu: University of Hawai'i Press, 2004.

Muan, Ingrid. "Citing Angkor: The 'Cambodian Arts' in the Age of Restoration 1918–2000." PhD dissertation. Columbia University, New York, NY, 2001.

Nelson, Roger. "Modernity and Contemporaneity in 'Cambodian Arts' After Independence." PhD thesis. University of Melbourne, Melbourne, 2017.

Nelson, Roger. "'The Work the Nation Depends On': Landscapes and Women in the Paintings of Nhek Dim." In *Ambitious Alignments: New Histories of Southeast Asian Art,* edited by Stephen H. Whiteman, Sarena Abdullah, Yvonne Low, and Phoebe Scott, pp. 19–48. Sydney and Singapore: Power Publications and National Gallery Singapore, 2018.

Nelson, Roger. "Phnom Penh's Independence Monument and Vientiane's Patuxai: Complex Symbols of Postcolonial Nationhood in Cold War-era Southeast Asia." In *Monument Culture: International Perspectives on the Future of Monuments in a Changing World,* edited by Laura Macaluso, pp. 35–48. Lanham, MD: Rowman & Littlefield, 2019.

Osborne, Milton. *Phnom Penh: A Cultural History.* Oxford and New York: Oxford University Press, 2008.

Pann Tra (romanised in the text as Pen Tra). "A Conversation with Pen Tra." In *Cultures of Independence: An Introduction to Cambodian Arts and Culture in the 1950's and 1960's,* edited by Ly Daravuth and Ingrid Muan, pp. 271–294. Phnom Penh: Reyum, 2001.

Phou Chakriya. "Thngai Min Rah" [The Sun Never Rises]. In *Gráp Yāng Doembī Anak Nā: Kamrang Snādai Aksārsilp Khmaer Paep Damnoeb / Who's It For?: Collection of Modern Cambodian Short Fiction,* edited by Teri Shaffer Yamada and Soeun Klo, pp. 66–80. In Khmer and English, with translation by NH Translation Group. Phnom Penh: Nou Hach Literary Association, 2014.

Polmuk, Chairat. "Invoking the Past: The Cultural Politics of Lao Literature, 1941–1975." Master of Arts thesis. Cornell University, Ithaca, NY, 2014.

Romey, Eliza. "King, Politician, Artist: The Films of Norodom Sihanouk." Master of Arts thesis. La Trobe University, Melbourne, 1998.

Sam Sam-Ang. "The *Pin Peat* Ensemble: Its History, Music, and Context." PhD dissertation. Wesleyan University, Middletown, CT, 1988.

Som Sophearin. *Bel Thngai Rah* [When the Sun Rises]. Phnom Penh: Angkor Thom, 2008.

Suon Sorin. *Brah Ādity Thmī Rah Loe Phaentī Cas* [A New Sun Rises Over the Old Land]. Phnom Penh: Wiriyeak, 1961.

Stewart, Frank and Sharon May, eds. *In the Shadow of Angkor: Contemporary Writing from Cambodia.* Honolulu: University of Hawai'i Press, 2004.

Thierry, Solange. *De La Rizière à la Forêt: Contes Khmers* [From the Rice Field to the Forest: Khmer Tales]. Paris: Editions l'Harmattan, 1988.

Yamada, Teri Shaffer and Soeun Klo, eds. *Gráp Yāng Doembī Anak Nā: Kamrang Snādai Aksārsilp Khmaer Paep Damnoeb / Who's It For?: Collection of Modern Cambodian Short Fiction.* Phnom Penh: Nou Hach Literary Association, 2014.

A New Sun Rises Over the Old Land

by Suon Sorin

First Published in Phnom Penh, 1961

Humbly dedicated
to the memory
of my father,
who worked tirelessly to raise me, exhorting me to be responsible and to
know right from wrong, while also reminding me to be steadfastly good.
He did not live to enjoy an independent citizen's right to freedom—a right
which was born of the achievements of His Majesty Norodom Sihanouk,
the Father of Independence, who is the principal architect of the policy of
neutralism and peace.

Preface

What prompted me to write this novel, *A New Sun Rises Over the Old Land*—since it was not the necessity of selling copies to earn a livelihood—was my wish to understand and to see the nature of Khmer compassion for Khmers, Khmer love for Khmers, people feeling pity for their own, and feeling love for their own.

According to my observations, most people oppress each other, are jealous of each other, and exploit each other; most people are not at all deserving of being called "people".

In my opinion, the many such terrible actions I have observed arise from one cause: money. Most people worship gold and silver more than any other god.

Silver and gold are just elements, not so different from a block of stone, but it is money alone that has the power to become the master over many thousands of people in this world of ours…. Most people willingly become slaves to money. Some people willingly sell their own body and honour for money.

And finally, there are some people who don't only strive to enrich themselves through honest means, but also choose to do immoral things for their own pleasure. These people fill their homes with pet cats and dogs, animals which sleep comfortably and eat well—much better than people like Grandfather Sok and Uncle Sav,[1] who work hard from early morning until night, but never earn much money…. People like Grandfather Sok and Uncle Sav have become workers, spending their whole lives working for other people, with no reward. Theirs is a life of earning a little in the morning, only to go without again in the evening. They never have enough for their exhaustion.

---

[1] In Khmer as in many other languages, it is common for honorific titles like "Grandfather" or "Uncle" to be used, outside of familial relations, to convey age and status. Sok and Sav are common Khmer names, seemingly used as generic examples here, rather than to refer to specific individuals.

The novel, *A New Sun Rises Over the Old Land,* is a story of the struggle between the horrible and the good; it is a story of the struggle between poverty and wealth; it is a story of the struggle between death and life. These are surely the struggles that we will encounter before long, if we are to realise our desires.

To write this book, I have needed nothing more than to observe that people have tolerance and compassion, and that people can love each other, including their own kind, without regard for status, class, ethnicity or race; without regard for whether someone is tall or short, big or small, rich or poor, black or white; and that people can live together in peace, working together to transform this world of ours into a new world, one which is abundantly glorious, according to the wishes of His Majesty Norodom Sihanouk, the leader of the government of Cambodia, who is the principal architect of the policy of peace.

Prologue

19 February 1960

The train carries its passengers out from the Battambang station and speeds toward Phnom Penh, reverberating and rumbling noisily, as if to shake the earth.

Most of the passengers are travelling together to the capital in order to join the Ninth National Congress. They are so happy, filled with indescribable joy. Some chat, others laugh gaily.

The first meeting of the Ninth National Congress will take place tomorrow…. The passengers all know this, and they hope that tomorrow will come quickly.

If we study these happy passengers very carefully, we will see a man who is big and tall. His skin is tan, his hair is curly, and his face is round. His eyes are sunken under thick, bushy eyebrows, and give the impression that this man is very precise in his work, but also has an active imagination.

This man is Suon Sam. He looks about twenty-eight years old. Suon Sam is wearing grey khaki trousers, and a white button-down shirt with long sleeves. He sits and smokes a cigarette, and as the smoke drifts away he casts his eyes across the landscape, examining it carefully through the train window.

* * *

That was at the end of the cool season. The cold air gusted in through the gaps in the train windows, as if it were trying to slice off the skin from the nose and ears of the people who lifted their faces to the window. Sam noticed the lush vegetation, which was green, radiant and fresh, as if to cheer on the journey of the people who were travelling to join the Ninth National Congress.

The sound of the wind as it blew through the drooping branches of the trees echoed thrillingly, musically, joyfully—the bright melody like a symbol of nature's perfection, enjoyed by all the people in the world. Everything was peaceful and pleasant. All along the journey, it was as if the trees and plants were competing to be the most joyous, sending a message to the cool season that it was almost time for it to end—because at the end of February all the vegetation begins to droop and wilt. The hot sun of the dry season would certainly come soon. Whatever happiness or regret humanity may feel, it is brought on by people, through their own actions....

Sam mused on the progress of the present, and on the damages of the past that were caused by a lack of security. Even the rice fields, the forests and the vast mountains are filled with the purity of life. The rice fields, forests and mountains are filled with a pure spirit, like the spirit of the Khmer ancestors from the era of Angkor. The rice fields, forests and mountains are so quiet and still, fresh and radiant with the colour and sound of nature.

Sam recalled the era of oppression for Cambodia, under French colonialism and imperialism; the era of insecurity for Cambodia; the era when all Cambodians lost their freedom amidst that insecurity; and the suffering and hardship that they endured.

He threw away his cigarette, then returned to his thoughts. Sam thought that....

Sam thought that the lives of all human beings are impermanent. But life's impermanence is the best possible lesson to show us the value of humanity, to teach us to be patient in the face of difficulty, or in the face of anything that goes against our wishes. The impermanence of life allows us to compare the good and the terrible, it helps us to judge whether humanity is good or terrible. Life's impermanence is like a witness, shedding light on the "new era", which we thought had ended long ago: exactly how was it different from our own time?

Our past lives have awakened us; they have prepared us to be more vigilant. Our past experiences have awakened us, and told us that we should not declare that justice is our destiny, for destiny is the only master over a life filled with hesitation and uncertainty, in which we cannot find the truth....

Destiny teaches us to know clearly that a good deed is not always what is needed. Because sometimes, a terrible action can be better than a good deed, too....

Sam thought very hard, and tried hard to understand what truly is a good deed, and what is a terrible one. Can anyone propose a theory of what constitutes a good deed, and what constitutes a terrible deed? It is always tricky. Say, for example, that we propose the theory that a good deed is like such-and-such, and we act according to this notion. Can we really be certain whether acting in this way will bring a truly good reward?

Sam swam in the abyss of this notion. In life, a good deed is not always rewarded with a good result for the person who commits that deed…. "Make merit, and receive merit" is a proverb that is easy to say, but difficult to really understand. Perhaps we must become wise before we can understand the depth of the proverb, "Make merit, and receive merit." Sam wondered, does an action need a kind of rhythm, in order to bring a good reward to the person who commits it? If that were so, then any theory of a good deed would become impossible to trust, because a good deed would become as if untrue. In that case, a good deed would be something that must be carried out in accordance with the time and circumstances, and only then can it reward the person who commits the good deed. But regardless, Sam still believed that a rhythm governs this life…. Every situation requires a rhythm, a pleasing tunefulness, like a music that is born of this rhythm. This is the truth of life; it is a truth that no one can refuse. Sam thought that he himself had known something of this rhythm…. It was a rhythm that made him laugh, even in his sorrow.

Thinking like this, Sam wanted nothing more than to scream and scream and scream! To scream in declaration of this new royal reign! To scream so that everyone might hear, so that the great weight of suffering that pressed on his heart might be lifted, at least a little.

Sam thought of his suffering as if it were a great ocean. That suffering was his life in the past, seven or eight years earlier. He had swum his way through it.

Sam thought of the happiness of this present time….

Dragging up his memory of life seven or eight years ago, and comparing it to his life in the present, Sam saw that his life in these two eras was as different as the sky and the land, as different as day and night. Before, Sam's life had been almost unbearable for him. But now, he had begun to achieve great success and happiness.

Thinking of his past, Sam wanted only to scream, to tell everyone. It had been a life completely filled with suffering and sadness.

And so, dear readers, I invite you to please read on. You will surely learn many tales of great suffering from Sam's past, as follows….

Chapter 1

The Family Line of Pitiful Farmers

The family line of Suon Sam is one of simple peasants. His ancestors on both the paternal and maternal sides were all rice farmers: rice farmers who only knew how to tend to the crops in the paddies. They are most deserving indeed of esteem and celebration, as the sowers of the seeds that feed the whole nation—but what farmer ever received such an honour? For rice farmers are the poorest of the poor, dressed in torn rags, without any education. During the colonial era, most rice farmers were looked down upon, disrespected and abused by the powerful and wealthy all across the countryside. And this continues today, because of the lingering remains of that colonialism. Whenever anyone is unhappy with someone, they invariably curse and call them a "damned farmer!" And besides that, farmers have sunk to being like slaves serving the capitalists or foreigners: people who are very cunning in the field of commerce.

Suon Sam is the only son of Mr Suon Sok and Mrs San, in the Bavel commune of the Sangker district, in Battambang province. In 1959, Suon Sok, Sam's father, was accused of being involved with the Khmer Issarak rebels.[2] French soldiers captured him, and took him to be tortured in Sdok Ach Romeas. Then they murdered him there, leaving Mrs San a poor widow. At the time Sam was still a student, only in the sixth grade. He bid farewell to

---

[2] Battambang province is commonly known as the "rice bowl" of Cambodia, as it is especially abundant for the cultivation of rice and other crops. The Khmer Issarak ("Independent Khmer") movement was a loose alliance of anti-French and anti-colonial rebels, active from the end of the Second World War. Bavel commune had been a significant site in their (and other) independence struggles. Sangker district had been the setting for a 1926 novel in French (*La Route du plus fort*) by George Groslier, an important scholar of Cambodian arts and culture, and founder of the art school and museum in Phnom Penh.

the classroom, that place for soaking up all kinds of knowledge and wisdom, and returned to work instead, to help his widowed mother.

One year later, the Issarak rebels suspected that Sam had become involved with the French. This terrified him, and made him very worried. He was forced to farewell his mother, who he loved as much as life itself, and journey to Battambang City, to escape from the Issaraks.

But that was a year of the most terrible misfortune for Sam: just four days after they separated, his mother died from a sudden illness. Sam returned to his hometown, to oversee her funeral. After the ceremony was completed, Sam—a cursed bachelor, who had just turned eighteen years old—resolved to make the journey to Phnom Penh, in search of work in the capital.

* * *

Sam had only one set of clothes left. He asked for a place to sleep with a monk in the Wat Mahamontrey temple.[3] A monk named Sav had offered his support, bringing Sam to work as a labourer in a trading business. He earned just fifteen riels a day.

This was the first time in his life that Sam had earned a salary. He had always thought that his future would be one of happiness and health. But as it turned out, everyone from the bosses to the sales agents who worked in the trading business looked down on Sam. It got to the point where he couldn't bear to work there any longer. The boss would curse Sam's mother and father if he was even just a tiny bit slow or late, or if he displeased them in any other way. Clerks would swear at Sam and call him names, making him feel totally belittled.

Sam had always believed that he should never stoop to become a slave to money, and that he should always maintain his humanity, and be equal to any other person. But the more he thought about it, the more he felt defeated. Poor people can never win! Conflicts in the age of French colonialism were so filled with horrific injustice. There was nothing more for Sam to do than to stop working in the trading business.

After that, he searched hard for another job. He tried asking for work in some government trading offices, but everywhere he went, the supervisors spoke harshly and cruelly to Sam. He couldn't bear their rude words, and so he often changed his place of work. He pitied his fellow workers, who had stooped to be the slaves of money! Workers who were sworn at and cursed, and who

---

[3] Wat Mahamontrey is a well-known Buddhist temple in central Phnom Penh.

were looked down on in every way, no different from animals. Sam's life took him to various other jobs … and finally, he fell into work as a *cyclo* driver.[4]

* * *

After that, Sam no longer slept at the temple, because he had a wife. Before they married, Soy, his wife, had worked as a servant for a capitalist. At Sam's suggestion, he and his poor wife rented a small hut, near the Psar Suon Thmei market.[5] It was the kind of place for workers who live hand to mouth, working in the morning in order to eat in the evening. As a *cyclo* driver, Sam had to pay a fee to the *cyclo* owner to rent the vehicle: it was thirty riels, every day.

Sam was the very poorest of the poor. On some days, he earned only enough money to pay the rental fee for the *cyclo*, and nothing more. Sam and his wife would go without eating in order to pay the rental fee, because the *cyclo* owner was the strictest of them all. She always gave the *cyclo* drivers a hard time, even if they did have the money to pay her. And any worker who didn't pay the fee, even just for one day, had to return the *cyclo* immediately, and had no hope of ever renting it again. It was always like this, because the capitalist *cyclo* owner had no pity for the workers at all.

---

[4] A *cyclo,* short for *cyclopousse,* is a three-wheeled vehicle, powered by cycling, similar to a pedalled rickshaw. First invented in Phnom Penh in 1937 and subsequently exported to the rest of French Indochina, the *cyclo* was a ubiquitous form of transport at the time when Suon Sorin was writing. Passengers sit in a covered seat, with the driver behind.

[5] Also known as Central Market or Psar Thmei, this is one of Phnom Penh's larger markets, built during the 1930s in an art deco style.

Chapter 2

The Life of a Worker in the City

In the middle of the monsoon season, the rain falls heavily, saturating the land almost every day. This makes it hard for *cyclo* drivers to earn any income, since there aren't many passengers. Sam had to use some of the money that he had saved to pay the rental fee for his *cyclo*—the *cyclo* that would soon wear him out completely.

The sky had been darkened with rain for three days already; it rained almost without stopping.

And this morning was soaked with rain again. Sam sat in their little hut, his arms wrapped around his knees. He was worried about his poor wife, Soy. There was nothing at all of any value in the hut, just a mat for the floor, a pillow, and an old mosquito net. The *cyclo* was parked in front. Sam's face was dark with worry. He hadn't been able to pay the rental fee yesterday. He wondered what they could do if the *cyclo* owner came to take away his vehicle…. It would be very difficult to find someone else to rent a *cyclo* from, because he would need a guarantor, and money for a deposit, too.

"What else can we do, Soy?" Sam asked his wife, sadly. "Perhaps you think I'm lazy, and stopped driving the *cyclo* just to enjoy myself? But I promise, I've been working so hard, hardly even stopping for a break, but there have been no passengers at all. And if the rain continues like this, there will *still* be no passengers, since people don't really go out in this weather."

Soy was a beautiful-looking woman. She was around seventeen years old, with a pretty, pale complexion and a good figure. She was a well-liked, quiet woman who didn't talk much, but was always honest with her husband.

Sam's words made Soy very upset. "No, my dear!" she replied. "I never think that you're lazy. Driving a *cyclo* is a risky job, and it's just bad luck to have no passengers! Today, you need to earn at least sixty riels to be able to pay the rental fee. You should hurry! If the madam who owns the *cyclo* comes, I'll lie and tell her that you've been unwell since yesterday, and couldn't take the rental fee to her. Please, my dear, hurry off!"

"Let's see how it goes today," Sam answered with a long sigh. "If I can't earn sixty riels, the madam owner will take the *cyclo* back for sure. And perhaps you and I will die from hunger, who knows?"

Soy sighed, and looked pityingly at her husband's face. "Give it a try, my dear. Maybe today you'll have better luck."

Sam smiled at his wife, and answered, "Yes, I'll go now, darling. I've done nothing but sit here while the rain falls, and it's almost noon already. If I come back a bit late tonight, please don't worry about me, okay?" He stood and walked out of the hut.

Sam drove away in the *cyclo* as the rain fell. Whenever there was heavy rain, the road in front of the hut would turn to deep and sticky mud. One of the front wheels of Sam's *cyclo* got stuck in a pothole; he had to get down from the seat and pull it from the front to get it out of the mud. At that moment, suddenly a car appeared. The driver's head emerged, and glared angrily at Sam, screaming, "Damn you! Why have you stopped your *cyclo* in such a stupid place? I almost crashed into it and killed you! Get out of here, quick! Sheesh, look,—I mean it!"

Feeling belittled, Sam tried to smile. From the way that this driver was talking and acting, it was clear that he looked on Sam with utter contempt. Sam wanted to answer rudely, but he stopped himself in time. "Oh!" he thought. "This is a rich man. If anything happens, I'll lose to him for sure." Thinking like this, Sam tried to stay quiet, and not say anything. He hurriedly pulled his *cyclo* out of the way to let the car pass. Then he jumped onto the seat and turned the vehicle away. And in that moment, Sam was suddenly stunned: he looked up and saw a woman standing with her hands on her hips in front of the coffee shop. It was Mrs Kim Leang, the wife of Mr Kim Chhun: a wealthy man who owned around 30 *cyclo* which he rented out, including the *cyclo* that Sam was driving.

Mrs Kim Leang was short and fat. She didn't bother to dress herself up much, but she loved money more than anything. This woman had a filthy mouth, and the meanest of all faces.

At that moment, Sam almost lost his senses; he was terrified that the woman would take the *cyclo* back, and deprive him of his livelihood. Seeing Mrs Kim in the middle of the road like this, Sam stopped his *cyclo*, and jumped off to beg for mercy.

"What the hell are you doing, damn you? This isn't like you! Why didn't you bring me the money for the *cyclo* yesterday?" As the woman spoke, her face was filled with a mean arrogance.

"Sorry, madam!" Sam answered, while lifting his hands in a *sampeah* gesture of respect.[6] "Yesterday I earned only ten riels. I'll bring the money to you this evening."

Mrs Kim Leang laughed cruelly, and said, "Damn you, you're all like this! Ugh, I'm so sick of doing business with the likes of you."

Sam lifted his hands in a *sampeah* once more. Mrs Kim Leang's manner of speaking was upsetting to his ears. "Damn, damn": they were harsh words, rude and disrespectful. All the workers who hired this woman's *cyclo* had to endure this kind of language from her.

"Go on then," the woman continued. "You've never done the wrong thing by me before. You told me that you couldn't earn the money, and I'll take a chance and believe you this time. But if you don't bring the money for me this evening, I'll send someone to take back my damned *cyclo*! There's nothing more to say, I won't waste my time to come and find you again. Damn it, I hate doing business with the likes of you!"

Although he was hurt by these words, Sam smiled. "Thank you so much, madam! This evening I will bring you the money."

"Ah, get out of here! I'm going." Mrs Kim Leang left.

Sam was terribly worried. He jumped back onto the *cyclo* and drove off immediately.

From the morning till noon, the rain poured down without stopping. Sam drove all over the city trying to find a passenger. He could earn only twenty riels, but he needed to pay sixty riels this evening! Thinking of this, Sam refused to take a break at all. He kept on driving his *cyclo*, and his eyes kept searching for a passenger to hail. He needed to earn at least sixty riels to pay the rental fee for the *cyclo*, but as for the cost of food for him and his wife, Sam wasn't so worried. In the house, they still had enough rice and *prahok* fish paste to eat for two or three more days....[7] He ate only so that he could live to drive his *cyclo*, not to enjoy the taste.

---

[6] The Khmer *sampeah,* a raising of two hands with the palms pressed together and fingers pointing upwards, is a gesture of respect commonly used as a polite greeting. It is similar to the Thai *wai,* or the Indian *namaste.*

[7] *Prahok* is a paste made from fermented fish, which is both a flavour enhancer, and a healthful probiotic food. Used as an ingredient in many Cambodian dishes, it is also eaten on its own with rice, especially during lean times, as it can be kept in storage for many months.

Sam drove down Ohyer Street. He was overjoyed when he saw a Chinese man raise his hand to call the *cyclo*. Sam hurried over to the man.

But … Sam had to slam on the brakes immediately, because there was a policeman nearby who ordered him to stop.

"Why are you riding in the middle of the road like that?" the policeman asked.

Sam's heart fell. The joy of finding a passenger had made him forget to watch the road, and he'd crossed the line by more than two metres.

Sam quickly jumped off the *cyclo*, and raised his hands in a *sampeah* to the policeman while apologising. "Please accept my apologies, sir. I wasn't looking."

The policeman's face was mean. He shook his head and answered immediately, "You damn people! You always have an excuse. The signal I made was loud and clear! How could you miss it?" The policeman spoke very strictly. "Look, bring me the *cyclo* licence book."

Sam politely passed the book to the policeman with both hands. This policeman had never forgiven anyone in his life. He carefully inspected the licence book, and then pulled out his own small notebook. When he saw this, Sam was terrified, because he knew that he would have to pay a fine of at least twenty-five riels.

"Your excellency!" Sam spoke with a shaky voice, his eyes looking pleadingly to the policeman. "Please kindly forgive me this time, sir!"

The policeman shook his head. "I have never forgiven anyone who did the wrong thing. You damn well know the rules, and when you break the law it is my duty to fine you!"

Sam was terribly distressed…. Driving a *cyclo*, he drenched himself in sweat just to earn a living, and even then it was usually not enough! Not only that, but he also had to be careful not to break the law, too, because if he came across a policeman he would have to pay a fine. Sam stopped pleading with the officer, and simply stood still and pretended to ignore him. When the policeman had finished writing out the fine, he passed it to Sam.

"Get out of here!" The policeman said. "Tomorrow you must go to Police Station Number Two."

That evening, Sam returned home a little before seven o'clock. In his shirt pocket, there was only thirty riels. His clothes were soaked in sweat. He was utterly exhausted, having ridden the *cyclo* from morning till night without finding any customers, and without earning enough money to pay the rental fee for the *cyclo*, either. And not only that, but the policeman had fined him, too! Soy sat waiting in the doorway of the hut, anxiously watching for her husband's return. When she saw the *cyclo* arrive, she rejoiced and quickly stood and rushed to meet her husband. Sam stopped the *cyclo* in front of the house, got off, and walked in despondently. From his facial expression, Soy knew immediately that he hadn't made enough money to pay the rental.

"Dear Soy!" Sam told his wife, "I made only thirty riels. What can we do? I feel terrible. And a policeman fined me as well—tomorrow morning I have to go to the station and pay at least twenty-five riels."

Soy was overcome with disappointment. "How did that happen? What did you do to make the police fine you?"

"I drove the *cyclo* onto the wrong side of the road."

Soy said nothing else. She brought her husband into the hut. Sam dropped to the floor, sat next to his wife, and hugged his knees to his chest, as was his habit.

"I think we're out of options! I don't know when we'll get to live easily like other people do." As he spoke, Sam looked at the food that his wife had served. There was nothing but one plate of rice, and one dish of *prahok* fish paste. Their lot in life left no room to breathe. And their biggest problem was the money that they had to go and pay tomorrow morning.

Sam sighed deeply. "The police fine is the most important thing, because if I don't pay that, I'll have to go to prison."

Soy opened her eyes wide. "Go to prison?" she asked in wonder.

"Of course!" Sam answered. "They'll bring me to prison if I don't pay the fine. Tomorrow I will beg the *commissaire*, and tell him honestly that I have only thirty riels. Perhaps he'll take pity and not fine me more than that. But as for this *cyclo*, even though it works perfectly well, I've lost hope that I'll ever be able to ride it again. I'll keep it here for the owner Mrs Kim Leang to take back. Even if I stay here to plead with her, she won't agree, because she is never lenient for anyone!"

Tears flowed from Soy's eyes. "Our time is up, my dear. I can't just sit here and do nothing. I have to find a way to help you to earn an income. I'll do any kind of work to earn some money to survive! You never let me go and work, or even just sell a few things here and there. But this time, please don't disapprove of what I will do. We must help each other to find an income. I can go and earn a wage anywhere, because these days there's nothing to be done at home."

Sam stroked his wife's back, gently and lovingly. Before he could answer her, he heard the sound of a woman shouting their names from in front of the hut. Sam felt a chill through his body, because he knew immediately that this was the voice of Mrs Kim Leang. He stood and walked out of the hut with a trembling heart, because Mrs Kim Leang was standing with her hands on her hips in an angry pose, with another man nearby.

"What the hell is this?" Mrs Kim Leang asked. "You promised you'd bring the money for the *cyclo* rental this evening. I waited for you until dark! I don't need to hear your damned excuses. Come! Give me the money! You damned people are all the same. None of you are any good, not one. You all owe me the money until I come to your house to take it. And then you claim that you're not feeling so well, or that your wife and child aren't well."

"I have no excuse, Mrs Kim Leang, other than to plead with you. I truly cannot find any income. Truly! Please, madam, please forgive me!"

Mrs Kim Leang raised her hand to silence Sam. "No! I can only take pity on those who pay the price of the *cyclo* rental. I bought these *cyclo* for tens of thousands of riels so that you could ride them. So what can I do? I need the money! If you don't have it, then stop riding my *cyclo*—you can go find someone else's to rent, go on! You people are terrible; you make some money then you just use it to gamble, or smoke marijuana, or drink alcohol. You never think about the owner of the *cyclo* at all!" When she'd finished speaking, Mrs Kim Leang turned to the man who was standing next to her. "Go on, Kuch! Take the *cyclo* back to the house!"

The man Kuch, her servant, obeyed her orders immediately, and she followed after him. Sam stood and watched them go, with tears flowing from his eyes. He gritted his teeth in silence for a moment, and then slowly began to speak. "Oh gods! Lord, you have no mercy on us poor people!"

Soy walked up close to her husband, and spoke. "My dear, whatever happens, we aren't starving to death yet. Even though they've taken the *cyclo* away, there are still other jobs we can do."

"Darling!" Sam spoke despairingly. "I've always stuck to an honest way of life. I've accepted poverty and hardship, but never agreed to do anything deceitful or illegal. But these good principles that I've lived by for so long haven't brought me any happiness at all! My dear, I want to become a thief. Perhaps that will make life a bit easier."

"Sam!" Soy protested. "Don't think like that! You should stick to the good way of life. Surely one day the gods will help us, surely."

Sam laughed in anger at their life, it was so dark and hopeless, without anyone to support them: no friends or relatives that they could depend on, and most of all, no money to spend. Must he suffer such hardships for his whole life?

"Go wash up and change your clothes," Soy said to Sam. "Then let's eat, and we can discuss how to make enough money to keep on living."

During such difficult times as these, Soy was the only one who could comfort Sam, and give him any sense of hope. He turned to his wife and said, "Darling Soy! I pity you so much. You should never have come to join in this suffering with me. Ever since we were married, we've encountered nothing but hardships. Sometimes we even go hungry."

"Sam! You should understand me better than that," she answered in a trembling voice. "My happiness doesn't come from money. It comes from loving and caring for you, and nothing else. I've told you many times: I could happily eat a block of salt, as long as I have your love."

Sam caressed his wife's shoulder, and smiled despairingly. "It's true, my dear. You are my heart and soul—there is nothing in this world that I love more than you, Soy. If I ever find a higher station in life than this, then I will gather all the happiness I can find and give it to you."

"My life and my body have been given to you," Soy replied. "I strive to be with you in suffering as in happiness, to be a good wife to you. My dear! Please don't think too much, it makes you sad and helpless. Please remember that the life of the poor people is always like this. We must grit our teeth, and never tire of struggling until the day we die. Today, we have escaped death, because we have rice to eat. Even that alone is something to be glad about. We shouldn't think yet of what we will do tomorrow—poor people have no future, because we can only live from day to day."

Sam nodded his head slowly, delighted by these rousing words from his poor wife. "My darling Soy, you're right. Life is struggle—so I must search hard for a new job."

Chapter 3

No Job and Nothing to Do

His beloved *cyclo*, that had shared so much misfortune with him, had been taken away by its capitalist owner, because Sam had failed to pay the rental fee for just two days. And so Sam had become a worker without a job. The very last money he had was just thirty riels, and even this he had used to pay a fine, because he had ridden his *cyclo* on the wrong side of the road.

A week passed. Anything in the hut that they could pawn, Sam had resigned himself to losing, in order to turn their lives around, and escape from the daily threat of death. Sam tried desperately to find a job. He went everywhere: to the shops, to the ports, to the warehouses, everywhere. But nowhere would agree to take him on. In some places, they yelled at him: "Do you have money to pay a deposit? If you have 500 riels to deposit, then tomorrow you can come to work!"

Every day, Sam returned to the hut feeling hopeless. One evening, just as he arrived back home, Sam ran into their landlord, an old man named Grandfather San. He owned many rental houses, but was completely without any sympathy for even the poorest people. Sam and Soy's neighbours knew that the capitalist old man would never agree for a tenant to delay their rental payment, not even by a day. In fact, the hut that Sam rented was one that Grandfather San had originally built as a temporary hut, when he first bought this plot of land. It was built as a hut for a guard to stay in, and when Sam went to rent it, Grandfather San profited in two ways: first, he had the rental income from the hut; and second, he didn't have to pay anyone to guard his land.

"What the hell, Sam!" Grandfather San spoke like someone who knows he can depend on the power of his money. "You used to pay your rent very reliably, but this month you're overdue by seven or eight days. What the hell are you thinking?"

Sam answered in gentle and respectful voice. "Please forgive me just this once, please!"

"Forgive? You mean you want me to give you some extra time to pay the rent, is that right?"

"Yes, sir."

"No! I cannot!" Grandfather San answered immediately. "I spent a lot of money to build this house, and I have to pay the taxes, too. You damn well need to understand: if you don't have the money to pay the rent, then you need to get the hell out of here!"

Sam lifted his eyes to look Grandfather San in the face, and smiled fearfully. "I have never done you wrong, sir. Please sir, please allow me just fifteen more days, sir."

"No! I cannot, damn you!" Grandfather San spoke very strongly. "I'll give you just one more day."

"Sir…." Sam spoke with a choking voice. Grandfather San had no desire to listen to Sam's pleading words. He hurried away from the hut. Sam watched the old capitalist walk away until he disappeared from view, then turned back to his wife, who was standing behind him.

"Darling!" Soy said to her husband. "If that's how it is, what are we to do?"

Sam gritted his teeth, feeling defeated by all the misfortune in his life. The way forward for them both seemed very dark, almost too dark to see. "My dear Soy! I'm at the end of my wits. The rent is 100 riels. Where can we get that from in time to give to him?"

Soy's eyes were despondent, as if she was about to cry. "So where can we go?" she asked.

"Wherever we are when night falls, we'll sleep there," Sam answered in frustration. "But I think we have no choice but to desperately struggle for our lives, until the day we die. Poor people like us have no hope of happiness, my dear."

"No matter how hard it is," Soy answered, "I know I will continue to bear it together with you."

Before he could say anything in reply, Sam heard the sound of a man calling his name. He turned and saw in front of him a handsome, well-dressed man, with a thin moustache running along his upper lip. The man was wearing fashionable clothes, with his hair combed neatly to one side, and he stood in front of Sam and Soy's hut. This young man's name was Sav, and to make a living, he was an expert thief. Sav was staying in a house near Sam's hut, with several young male friends. He had plenty of money to throw around, and wore only the most expensive clothes. Sav had chosen to rent a house in this neighbourhood because it was quiet, and because most of the people here were workers who would spend every evening only what little money they'd earned that morning. There was no one around here who would care to notice what it was that Sav did for a living. Sam called out, and went out to greet the young man. Sav smiled through his moustache, and patted Sam lightly on the shoulder.

"How are you, Sam? What did you do to make Grandfather San carry on so loudly? You owe him the rent, do you?"

Sam nodded his head, and before he could say anything, Sav took him by the hand and led him over to sit down at his house. Sav encouraged Sam to chat about this and that, while several of his friends left to go to work in the market.

"Hey, Sam!" Sav said. "I really pity you, you know. Now you've stopped driving a *cyclo*, right?"

"Yeah, Sav," Sam replied. "I owed the *cyclo* rental fee, and the owner came and took it away."

"So what are you doing for work these days?"

Sam laughed ruefully. "I'm looking for a job. I'll do anything, as long it's honest work."

"Oh, Sam," Sav said with a smile. "You're so stupid! So stupid that there's nothing I can do to help you. I've invited you many times to come and make money like I do. It's so easy. Even on a bad day you can make 100 riels, and on a good day you can make thousands—just imagine! We're poor people, if we spend our time thinking about honour and goodness, then we'll starve to death. You think about it, Sam! Money is a god…. It is the jewelled chalice. People always say that rich people are good, and poor people are bad. If you have money, then everyone respects you and honours you as a good person, but the way you are these days, no matter what kind of morality you have, you cannot avoid the wealthy people looking down on you. They always think that they're superior, and that a poor person like you is just the slave beneath their feet. Oh, Sam! The capitalists and the excellencies, most of them build their happiness and their power on the backs of the poor. They rob the Khmer people and they rob the Khmer nation. The way I see it, we should go and steal all of that back. I really like your quiet character, Sam. And now you have no work, so I want to want to invite you to make some money with me."

Sam smiled fearfully at Sav. "Thank you very much, Sav, for wanting to help me like this. But I can't do what you do…."

"Because you have these stupid ideas about morality, right? It's for nothing, Sam. No one sees the morality of the poor. There is no job that can make money like thieving—these days, I live happily and I eat well, and I have nice clothes that I can wear to watch the movies in any cinema."

"Your happiness and mine are very different, Sav," Sam answered. "You are happy with a life of thieving, but I'm happy with having an honest job. No matter how much the work makes me sweat, I'm still happy to do it. Let me tell it to you straight: in my life, I will never do anything dishonest or illegal."

"Well, that's up to you, Sam," said Sav. "If you're happy to starve to death, then go ahead. But as for me, I can do anything if it makes money."

"But your work is very dangerous."

"That's true, Sam," Sav answered. "Do one thing wrong, and I'll go to jail immediately. But for people like me, jail is not such a big deal. I've been to jail before, and in a way, it's easy, too: when it comes time to eat, there's a meal prepared for you, and there are people to guard you, too." When he'd finished speaking, Sav put his hand in his pocket and pulled out 100 riels to show off to Sam. "Look at this, Sam! I left the house for just a moment and made almost 2,000 riels while a shopkeeper was distracted going to buy a movie ticket. Think about it! Two thousand riels in one day!"

"Sorry, Sav," Sam said. "I can't do what you do. I'm stupid, just like you said. I'm determined to starve to death instead of doing something dishonest. So that's it! Goodbye Sav…."

Sav shook his head. "Go and sleep on it for a night, my friend! If you agree to work with me, I'll buy some nice new outfits for you to wear, and give you some money to spend so that you have nothing to be embarrassed about. Ever since I gave the landlord 100 riels a year ago, he still doesn't dare to open his mouth to me. Because he knows that even if the rent goes up to 1,000 riels, I'll still get it for him…."

Sam had nothing more to say, and he stood and walked out of Sav's house, not knowing what to think.

The next evening, Sam and Soy met the callous capitalist Grandfather San again. Sam wasn't feeling very well, since returning home from looking for work and finding nothing, just like on every other day. But he tried hard to smile for his landlord, and pleaded with him to give them an extension. Sam even pointed out how poor they were, so that the landlord would understand, but the only response from Grandfather San was a barrage of curses.

"Your poverty is not my concern!" Grandfather San said harshly. "I cannot help you. All I need is the money you owe me for rent, there's no need for you to explain anything more than that. If you don't have the money, then you have to get out of my house! In fact, I should take the rent that you owe me for these past seven or eight days, too. But I won't take it, just as long as you leave this evening."

Sam almost couldn't bear it. He tried to look at Grandfather San, and even though he was furious, tried to plead with him once again.

"Sir, you should take pity on poor people like me, sir. Ever since I arrived, I have never paid you the rent late even once, until this time. I beg of you, sir...."

Grandfather San laughed angrily. "If I spent my time pitying people like you, I might never make a living! If I'm not strict with people like you, then in the future no one will pay their rent to me. I have nothing more to say to you. Give me the money, or don't; it's up to you."

"Please give me another half a month, sir."

The old capitalist shook his head, and said forcefully, "I told you already, I cannot. So now will you give me the money or not?"

"Sir!" Sam said, his voice shaking. "I don't have it yet, sir."

"If that's the case, then you have to get out of my house! Get out tonight."

It was too much, Sam couldn't bear it. He said nothing more to Grandfather San, and the old man walked away.

Sam thought that it was surely true that poor people like him had no chance to argue with rich people, because money was more powerful than anything, even honour. And whenever money was involved, it could be used unjustly, too.

Sam sighed deeply while he looked at his wife. Then he told her to pack up their things so that they could leave Grandfather San's hut.

Since they had no other option, that evening Sam took his wife to sleep out in the open, under the eaves of the Vietnamese monks' quarters in the Wat Toul Prosrey temple. Sam had no belongings other than a mosquito net, a pillow, a mat to sleep on, and two changes of clothes for himself and his wife. What's more, Sam and Soy had with them just ten riels, which was the very last money they had to keep them alive. Now, they were trapped without a home, no different from beggars.

The atmosphere in the Wat Toul Prosrey temple was quiet and deserted, and it felt very lonely. Sam and Soy sat hugging their knees to their chests, looking sorrowfully at one another. In front of the western corner of the temple, there were two or three dogs lying lazily at the end of a leash. Sometimes they snarled, sometimes they barked, and sometimes they attacked each other.

Five days passed! Five days that passed in sadness and sorrow for Sam and Soy.

One evening, Sam was fast asleep and snoring loudly on their torn mat. Near him was a small basket.

It was seven o'clock already. Soy was rushing through the gate toward the temple, carrying in her hands a packet of rice and food that she'd bought at the market. Her expression was more cheerful than usual.

As soon as she set foot into the temple grounds, Soy called out to her husband. Sam woke, then got up and looked curiously at his wife.

"Gosh! It's so late," Sam said sleepily. "When did you go to the market? I didn't realise. I was just lying there thinking, then suddenly I fell into a deep sleep."

Soy put the package of rice and food on the tiled floor, and sat down close to her husband, smiling at him. Then she told Sam that when she'd been at the market, she'd met an old lady. This old lady was looking for a woman to work for her boss, a man named Hok, to do the cleaning and take care of his house. Soy explained that she had already agreed to go and live with him, because he would give a salary of 200 riels each month. Tomorrow, Soy would meet with the old lady, so that she could bring her to meet the boss, Hok.

Sam listened to his wife, and sighed. "Soy, my dear, I don't want you to be separated from me. But what can we do? Now, it's like we're beginning to drown already. We have no choice but to live separately for a while. If you can really earn an income by staying with them, then I think I'll travel to the countryside for five or ten days, too, since now it seems as though the Issarak rebels have quietened down a bit. I'll go and sell some things in the countryside, maybe make some money to bring back and go into business with someone."

Soy looked at her husband, and asked doubtfully, "But dear, where will you get the money for a train ticket?"

"Don't worry about that!" Sam replied. "We still have one mosquito net we can sell, and if I'm a bit short, I'll go and borrow a bit of extra money from a friend…. Oh, and tomorrow, I'll take you to Hok's house. If he's generous, I can ask to sleep there too, and I'll happily do any work he demands, if I can stay close to you."

Sam and Soy looked at each other and smiled. "Darling," Soy said. "Please don't worry. Even if you can't stay and work there together with me, no matter where you go, I'll ask the boss to let me go and see you at least once a week."

"Oh! When will we be able to enjoy life like other people do?" Sam cried out.

Soy undid the package of rice and food, and shared it between them. They ate in silence, filled with a feeling of sadness.

The next morning, the old woman that Soy had met at the market came to bring her to meet the boss, Hok. Sam took the opportunity to go along too, so that he'd know where the house was, and so that he could ask for a job, too.

Hok was a middle-aged man, a trader with piles of money. He was a widower, and even though he was about forty years old, he still looked young and fit, because he was rich. Hok's house was big and spacious, with two or three cars, and more than ten servants, both men and women. To an outsider, Hok seemed like a good man. He was of Chinese background, but he didn't behave like a Chinese man. Hok was a person who everyone knew and liked, just because of the power of his money.

From the very first moment that he saw Soy's face, Hok was delighted by her appearance. But he didn't like Sam at all, once he knew that he was Soy's husband.

"I agree to take you on as my woman-servant immediately," Hok said. His conduct seemed to be nothing but kind and generous. "To begin with, I'll give you a salary of 200 riels a month, but as for your husband, I'm very sorry but I don't have anything suitable for him to do. But if he ends up visiting you often, then maybe I'll find something for him to do."

These very kindly words, although they came from a heart that was most cruel and slovenly, were enough to win Sam's total respect for this capitalist Hok. Sam held Hok in the highest esteem, even though he had the heart of a thief. His words were enough to make Sam have hope that in the future, his wife would find happiness under the roof of this capitalist's house….

"I'm delighted!" Sam said, in the most respectful of terms, while lifting his hands in a *sampeah* gesture of respect to Hok. "I'll be glad to send my wife to you, your excellency."

"Don't worry! Don't worry! I always have nothing but kindness and compassion for all of my servants, as if they were my own children."

Before Sam and Soy parted, she walked with him to the outside gate. They looked at each other with passionate desire. "Soy, my dear! Please work hard to truly serve his lordship, you hear me?" Sam told his wife. "This man seems very kind, and not at all snobbish."

"So when are you going to the countryside? When you get back, please come to see me right away, yes?"

"I want to go tomorrow, and I'll go for just seven or eight days. I'll be back. Goodbye, my dear!"

Sam and Soy separated from each other while filled with desire. Sam walked away from her, but in his mind he still saw nothing but Soy….

Chapter 4

Under the Roof of the Capitalist's House

Just one day after coming to stay under the roof of the boss Hok's house, Soy was already terrified.

Many of the other female servants told Soy in whispers that Hok behaved most outrageously with women. Almost all of them had fallen into his trap, becoming like food for Hok's enjoyment.

While Soy was alone, sweeping and cleaning the small room behind the room she would be sleeping in, Hok went in and confronted her face to face. He wouldn't stop staring at her. No matter how he smiled at Soy, she was terrified, because she remembered what the older female servants had said earlier that day....

"Soy!" The boss Hok said with a smile. "What is it about you that makes me pity you so?"

That night, not more than two or three hours after dark, Hok schemed to rape his poor servant, Soy. She was as helpless as an eggshell in his claws.

It was nine o'clock.... The rain was falling heavily....

Soy was sitting and worrying in her bedroom alone, filled with sadness. She was thinking of her beloved husband, and of her own poverty and despair and misfortune.

At that moment, Soy heard the sound of someone knocking at her door. She felt a tingling down her spine, and shrank back in fear from whatever was going to happen, just like the older women-servants had told her it would....

"Who is it?" she called out in a small and shaking voice.

"It's me!"

Soy felt a trembling in her stomach when she heard Hok's voice. She stood up, and froze for a moment, before resolving to go and open the door. She thought, if her boss was planning to rape her, she would raise her hands and offer him a *sampeah* gesture of respect, and plead with him, to try to escape from this danger.

The door opened, and suddenly Soy was face to face with Hok. "What are you doing, Soy?" he asked with a smile.

"Oh, I'm not doing anything, sir."

Hok walked right up to her, and she backed away from him. Her heart almost stopped beating, and he kept on coming closer and closer. Soy's face was white, drained of blood. She wondered what on earth could she do. This was a terrible situation she was entangled in….

The rain kept on falling incessantly. Soy edged back against the wall and stood motionless. She saw what Hok's intention was.

"Soy!" Hok spoke as he continued to come closer to her.

Her body shook in terror, like a fawn in front of a lion. "Sir," she said in a trembling voice, while raising her hands in a *sampeah*. "Please sir, take pity on me…."

Hok smiled. He was so thrilled by Soy's figure; her soft flesh made him burn with lustful desire. Hok found his happiness in being intimate with women who he enjoyed—even if those women were his servants. He didn't care whose wife or daughter these women were. He rubbed gently on Soy's shoulder. "Don't be afraid, Soy! Come, sit with me and chat for a bit."

"Sir!" Soy replied. "If you don't need me for anything tonight, please sir, wait to discuss it with me tomorrow!"

Hok laughed quietly, and grabbed Soy's hands, pulling her to sit on the bed near to him. "Don't be afraid of me, Soy! I won't do anything to you. I just came to chat with you, since I am so pleased with your behaviour."

"But I'm your servant; it's not appropriate for someone of your status, sir."

"Don't worry about that, Soy! Don't think about that. I'm not an ogre— come and sit with me! Sit and chat with me, I'm no snob."

Hok sat on the bed, and pulled Soy closer to him. He reached into his pocket and pulled out two brand-new 100 riel notes, and pushed them into Soy's hands. "Ah, Soy! Take these 200 riels, go on." Hok embraced Soy with a sudden urgency. "Soy, don't be afraid. Don't worry so much. You will be very happy if you agree to be my wife, because your face makes me pity and love you so."

Soy sobbed. Her entire body shook in terror. She pushed the money back to her boss. "Please sir, take your money back. Take it to buy whatever you need with another woman. I'm not available, I have a husband already."

Hok looked at Soy in irritation. "Soy! You are poor. Do poor people not need money? Let's be together for just a moment. There's no one to see or to hear, and you'll get 200 riels right away."

Soy had never realised that a rich man of such high status could be so horrible, so coarse, and so immoral. She had never imagined that he could throw away any sense of shame or decency in the name of seeking sexual pleasure, with no thought that the woman he was with was someone else's wife, someone else's daughter.

"Sir! I cannot be your wife," Soy said tearfully. "I came to this house to be your servant, to earn your money. Even though I'm poor, I still know right from wrong, and good from bad. I am always faithful to my husband."

Hok grabbed her, and hugged her close to him once more. Soy struggled free, and stood up. She no longer had any respect or esteem for her boss.

"Sir!" she continued. "Please understand that not all poor people are the same. Sir, please understand that the power of your money is no use with a poor person like me. I came here to earn an income from you because I'm poor. But I'm happy only to live morally. I'd rather die than give my body to you. I'll leave this house of yours right now. I never realised that a rich person like you could be so utterly horrible."

Hok lunged at her, and blocked the doorway. His face, which had been smiling just a moment ago, was now scowling in anger. "Soy!" he said, furiously. "You have fallen into my trap already. You can't escape. I need you, my darling…. You're not going anywhere!"

He came up close to her again. Soy tried to scream, but the rain was falling very heavily outside, and Hok's hand was very quick to cover her mouth. Together, the rain and his hand meant that her voice couldn't be heard outside of the room. This capitalist, who looked at this poor woman like she was nothing more than some tasty food for him to devour, lunged forward and grabbed Soy again, and bent down to kiss her with a passionate lust. She struggled to free herself from Hok's barbarity, but as she was a woman, there was nothing she could do to find the strength to escape. Finally, Soy resigned herself, and fell into Hok's arms. He carried her, with fearsome strength, and put her down on the bed….

That night, Soy was shaking with terror. She had once sworn that she would never allow herself to be called a woman who has two husbands. But that night she had lost everything to this rich man, who always sought his pleasure from the women-servants in his house.

* * *

The next morning, Soy left Hok's house very early. She almost killed herself out of sorrow. Soy felt that the one thing that was the most valuable in her life had been ruined, and that the foul stench of Hok's lust would follow her for as long as she lived…. She cried until her eyes were swollen. And she left Hok's house without saying goodbye to anyone.

Soy went to find her friend who drove a *cyclo*. He was close to her husband, and they used to help each other, like brothers. The man's name was Mey, and his wife was Mom. They were both very friendly, and they greeted Soy warmly, like always. Soy told Mey and Mom the terrible tale of what had happened in Hok's house the night before. She told them everything, and then she asked if she could stay with them for a while, until her husband came back from Battambang.

Mey was very understanding. "No problem, Soy!" he said. "Our house is like your house too. Sam used to come and sleep here sometimes, and once in a while he even plucked up the courage to ask to borrow some money. Just yesterday, I had 200 riels, and I let Sam borrow 150 riels. He told me he was going to Battambang for five days. He'll be back soon. Don't worry, Soy, you can stay with us until then."

Soy stayed with Mey and Mom from then on. She helped Mom with the housework, cooking meals, watching the two children, and so on.

Five days passed. On Thursday evening, the train from Battambang to Phnom Penh arrived to the capital, with Sam on board, at two-thirty in the afternoon. Sam had come back to Phnom Penh very pleased with his successes. He had gone to collect some debts that were owing to him, and also sold some things. Now he had 600 riels.

Sam hurried to Hok's house to find his wife, to tell her that their fate was a little more promising than before. He also planned to tell her that he would allow her to stay to earn an income from Hok for only one month, and then she would stop, and come back to Sam so that they could be together and take care of each other.

Sam arrived to Hok's house at three o'clock. One of Hok's woman-servants told Sam that Soy had stayed for just one night, and then had disappeared early the next morning. They had heard the boss saying that Soy had stolen many of his things.

Sam was shocked. He couldn't believe that his wife would dare to steal from Hok. But then he remembered how poor they had been, and how difficult everything was then. Sam realised that sometimes things like this really did happen, especially since Soy wanted to help with finding money. He didn't ask any more questions, but quickly said goodbye to this woman-servant, and hurried away.

Sam had just a few close friends who were workers. He thought that for sure Soy would have gone to stay with one of his friends, so he hurried off to find his wife. The first house that he went to was Mey and Mom's.

When Sam arrived at their house, Mey was driving his *cyclo* out, preparing to go and earn some money by bathing himself in sweat as if it were water....

The two of them had a mutual feeling of closeness and affection. "Brother Mey!" Sam called out. "As soon as I got off the train, I went to see my wife at Hok's house, but she wasn't there. A woman-servant told me that my wife had stayed in that house for just one night, and had stolen from Hok and run away. And now I don't know where she is."

Mey gritted his teeth. "She didn't go anywhere. Soy is here in my house."

Mey went on to tell Sam the whole terrible story, in the very words that Soy had used to tell them.

Sam stood motionless and transfixed, as if a bolt of lightning had struck him right in the chest. Tears fell from his eyes, the tears of a poor man who had been caused pain by a rich one.... "That Hok!" Sam said hatefully. "I cannot just let this be. If he dares to rape my wife, then I must dare to kill him too!"

Mey patted Sam on the shoulder, and interrupted him. "No, Sam! Don't go to interfere in his affairs. He's a rich man, you must realise that this is your fate...."

Sam rushed into the house. His heart pounded in his chest when he saw that Soy was sleeping, wrapped in a blanket. Sam called out to his wife, loud enough to wake her. As soon as she saw her husband, Soy began to sob. Sam went and sat close to her, and softly caressed her forehead, and spoke comfortingly to her. "My darling, don't cry! Mey told me everything. Don't worry my dear. I will get revenge on him for this horrible act.... I have no choice but to kill him."

"No, dear! Don't! Don't think like that. If you try to get revenge for me, then you'll go to prison for sure! Don't do anything. This is our fate."

Sam was filled with a violent hatred. No matter what Soy, Mey or Mom did to try to stop him, he refused to put aside his murderous intention to kill Hok.

Mey said, "Don't worry, Sam. It's so difficult for Soy. You can stay here until you find a house to rent."

Sam smiled through his tears, but his heart was filled with rage.

Chapter 5

In Prison After Falling for the Capitalist's Trick

The rain was drizzling lightly.... Flashes of lightning sent momentary bursts of brightness, and the thunder rolled on.

That night, Sam was determined to go and kill the capitalist Hok, who had menaced his wife in a fit of lust, causing Soy a lifetime of suffering and shame.

Sam had entered Hok's property, inside the perimeter fence. His clothes and body were soaked with rain. He stood in the dark, in the shadow of a big tree behind the house. Sam held a dagger in his hand, and it was this knife that he planned to drive into the chest or the stomach of the evil, wicked capitalist Hok, who had forced himself on Sam's wife....

The electric lights in Hok's house were still on. Sam stood still in silence for almost half an hour. Finally, he saw Hok pacing in his room.

Sam's expression was terrifying. His eyes were red like burning coals. He guessed that the room that Hok was walking back and forth in was his office. Sam slowly edged closer to the house, fearful of anyone seeing him before he'd been able to kill this devilish capitalist.

Sam guessed right. The room above was Hok's office. He was wearing house clothes, and smoking a large pipe. He was busy thinking about business; his desk was covered in various documents.

Hok was pacing back and forth inside the room. After a while, he sat down on a chair at his desk. At that moment, Sam scrambled to climb up to the window on Hok's left, and edged slowly in through it. He stood still for a moment, looking sideways at Hok. Then he spoke, in a strong, clear voice.

"Mr Hok!"

Hok jumped in surprise, and turned to see where the voice came from. When he saw that it was Sam, Hok was shocked. He knew immediately why

Sam had invaded his house, and why he was holding a dagger in his hand. Sam had not come for any good reason. The shameless capitalist was terrified, like any rich man would be, having committed terrible crimes and fearing death.

Hok's situation was helpless. He stood in shock for a moment, and then tried to smile to Sam, with an expression of pleading. "Ah, it's you Sam! Why have you come here?"

"Yes! It's me, sir," Sam said, using respectful terms. "That's right, my name is Sam. You remember me, do you, sir? We've only met once, but you still remember me, of course, since I'm Soy's husband…."

Hok's face was white. Beads of sweat were forming on his forehead. His life was in Sam's hands. His eyes were wide, and as red as blood; his flesh tingled, and he wondered in terror what he could do to control Sam.

"Sam!" Hok said, trying to calm himself. "What are you doing, Sam? Sit down. Can't this wait until tomorrow, then you can come to see me? You shouldn't go out in the rain like this."

Sam laughed cruelly. "Sir!" he said, looking as if he was about to rip into Hok. "Make no mistake, sir, I am here to take your life! To kill you in exchange for all that you ruined in my wife with your savage actions. Sir! You are a rich man, and you think that a poor woman is just a plaything, just entertainment to make you happy, like a flower in your hands. You never stopped to think that this woman is someone else's wife! Soy is my wife, she is my heart, and I love her more than life itself. I love her like any man loves his wife—and this is why I've come to you, sir, to take your life with this dagger. Don't scream, sir! Please be still…. There's no use in screaming, sir, because you have sealed this room tightly, and locked it from inside too. Even if someone did come to help you, this dagger is sharp and it will pierce right into your heart."

When he'd finished speaking, Sam edged closer to Hok. Whimpering, Hok backed away. He was terrified, and in his terror, he lifted his right hand, and begged in a trembling voice: "Stop! Stop, Sam! Calm yourself for a moment. Before you kill me, please take a moment for me to say something."

Sam stood directly in front of Hok. He was like a crazed ogre. His loathsome smile terrified the capitalist. "If you want to say something to me, sir, please say it quickly," Sam ordered. "I will only give you a few minutes, and that's it."

Hok's heart almost stopped beating in terror. "Sam! I've done the wrong thing, I've gone too far," he begged. "I don't dispute that I took your wife. But I did that, I went too far, because I was drunk. I didn't know what I was doing, I didn't know wrong from right…."

"Sir!" Sam spoke after he laughed with anger. "Sir, you are not a savage. You are a rich man, with a good education. As for me, I'm just a worker, so how is it that I know about responsibility? Whatever you do, you try to explain away, but your words aren't enough for me to forgive you. I've made up my mind. I must kill you sir, and nothing will change my mind...."

"Stop, Sam! Stop!" The capitalist begged him, and lifted his hands in a *sampeah* gesture of respect to the worker. "If there is any way that I can repay you for this mistake, please take pity and tell me, Sam! Whatever happens, your wife has given her body to me already, and there is no use in you killing me. You will just be put in jail and locked in chains, Sam! If you are willing to go to jail, then do you not care about your wife at all? Sam! Wouldn't it be easier to take my money? I'd be happy to give you my money right now; it's up to you how much. Whatever you want, I'll give it to you right now. Wouldn't that be more useful than killing me, Sam?"

"Sir! My wife is not something that you can buy!" Sam interrupted. "Your savage actions, sir, have put a wound in my wife's heart which will remain there forever, until the day she dies."

Hok seemed more hopeful, when he saw that Sam's words were a little more gentle than before. "My brother!" Hok said. "I have done the wrong thing. Let me repay you for my terrible action with money. Go on! Please don't think that I look down on you, not at all. In fact, you're a poor person, you should take this compensation from me, and use it as capital to do some business. You and your wife will be happy from now on. So tell me, Sam, how much money do you need?"

Tears flowed from Sam's eyes. He stood, motionless, for a moment; the power of money had made him hesitate. In the life of a poor person like him, Sam thought, there was never a time to hope for any prosperity. Life was nothing more than eating in the evening with whatever he'd earned in the morning: it was the same, over and over again. Sam thought that if he took 10,000 riels as compensation from Hok, that would be enough to bring some happiness to him and his wife.

Poor people are always and inevitably enslaved to the power of money.... In this world, those who have food to eat, those who can live how they like, can surely only do so because of money.

Sam looked at Hok from the corner of his eye, showing his submission. "Sir! If I take this compensation from you, you'll probably just think that I'm asking too high a price for my wife's body, won't you? Since she's poor, I mean."

Hok smiled, because he knew he'd won.

"No, my brother! I don't think like that," Hok replied. "It's up to you, you can name whatever price that is fitting for how much you love your wife. So tell me! How much money do you need?"

"Ten thousand riels!" Sam answered immediately.

Hok nodded his head in agreement.

"Okay, my brother, okay! I'll get the money for you right away."

"Thank you very much, sir," Sam replied. "But please give it to me now, don't go anywhere…."

"Oh, my brother!" Hok interrupted. "I'm not tricking you. I pity you! And I'm happy to give you 10,000 riels right away."

Hok smiled at Sam. He went over to his desk, and opened the right hand drawer. In that moment, the attitude of this thieving capitalist suddenly changed. He pulled out an eight millimetre revolver from the drawer, and pointed it at Sam. And then he laughed happily, in the manner of a rich man who has won.

"Drop your knife, Sam! Now!" Hok shouted. "If you want to live, then don't move! I told you to drop your damned knife, you hear me? If you don't do as I say, I'll kill you right now. This is my house, and I have the power to shoot you like a dog. Damn fools like you are too stupid to think. Who the hell would agree to give you 10,000 riels, Sam? Your wife isn't worth more than ten riels. Drop your knife right now, you idiot!"

The dagger fell from Sam's hand. The gun had defeated him. He glared at Hok, without blinking; Sam's eyes revealed the murderous rage that filled his heart.

Hok walked backwards to the door. He turned the handle, opened it, and called out for a servant to come. Right away, a woman-servant entered. Seeing Hok pointing his gun at a man she didn't know, the woman-servant was terrified. The capitalist yelled at her to go and fetch three or four male coolies from the back of the house to come quickly and help to tie Sam up.

"Go on, kill me, Hok!" Sam said.

"Now I've got you!" Hok replied, laughing at his victory. "Sam, it's a real shame! The bullets in my gun are worth more than your life. Poor people like you have no value. I'm going to have my servants drag you away by the neck and take you to the police, that'll be better. You know that you'll go to prison for many years, don't you, for trying to kill me? But I'll tell them to go a bit easy on you, since I took your wife that time. I'll only accuse you of breaking into my house, so you'll only need go to prison for three months at the most. That'll be a lesson for you, to think ahead more next time. There was no way you could beat me, Sam! No way at all."

Sam gritted his teeth, and imagined what it would be like in prison. A great misery had befallen him. Sam had fallen under Hok's control, and he saw that there was no way to escape from his authority.

Three servants hurried into the room. Hok was delighted. "Watch out! This damned guy broke into my house. Tie him up and take him to the police! But you should rough him up a bit first."

The three servants immediately rushed over and grabbed Sam, just as their boss had told them to. He tried to protect himself, but the sound of Sam falling to the floor echoed through the house. The capitalist stood and smiled happily as he watched the struggle of one man against three. The servants attacked Sam, getting him right in his bones, and he fell flat on the floor. They surrounded him and kicked him until he was beaten all over.

"Hey! That'll do!" Hok yelled. "Drag him off to the police now. Tell them that you saw him breaking into the house, then that you chased and caught him, but that he fought back and that's why you had to beat him. Make sure you plan it and all say the same thing to the police!"

The biggest of the coolies raised his right leg and kicked Sam once more. He collapsed, falling onto his face. The electric lights were on, so they could clearly see Sam's face: his right eye was swollen, and his mouth was bleeding.... Hok's top servant bent down, grabbing Sam's hair to make him stand up. His legs were weak and shaky, almost too weak to hold him. The poor, unlucky worker was almost out of breath, but his eyes were still open, glaring at Hok.

Another of Hok's closest servants laughed cruelly, and grabbed at Sam's shirt, jerking him with all his strength and making him fall backwards into the wall. Another man rushed over and kicked him once more. Sam doubled over in pain, collapsing in front of Hok, who was still laughing at his success. The servants tied Sam up and took him to the police, who then took him off to be held in the Kuk Thom prison.[8]

Not long afterwards, Sam was taken to court, and the judge sentenced him to three months in prison.

---

[8] Kuk Thom was a notorious prison established during the colonial period, located in central Phnom Penh.

Chapter 6

Terrible Suffering in the Kuk Thom Prison

Sunday was the day when the authorities allowed families to visit prisoners. Soy prepared a small package of cakes, and went to ask for permission to visit her husband, along with Mey. She sobbed out of pity when the prison guard brought Sam out to meet her, and she saw the terrible fate that the thieving capitalist had inflicted on him....

"My darling! You're chained up in prison because of me!" she said, with tears flowing from her eyes. "I told you not to hold a grudge, and not to do anything to him! He's a rich man, and this is what happened when he didn't even accuse you of trying to kill him. So don't do anything else, or you'll be in prison for ten years more!"

"Yes, dear," Sam replied. He looked at his wife with a feeling of desire. "Now it's gone too far! Don't worry, I can bear my fate. Three months isn't so long." Sam turned to Mey. "Brother Mey! Please take care of my wife. There's no one I trust as much as you."

"Of course, Sam," Mey replied kindly. "Soy will stay with us, and we'll be responsible for her."

Sam was greatly comforted by Mey's compassion. "Mey! You're so good to me," he said. "Even though I'm poor and struggling, you don't forget me. I'll remember your kindness, my friend."

Soy gave the package of cakes to her husband. Before any of them could say anything else, a guard came over and yelled at them. "That's it! That's enough talking."

Sam stood and said goodbye to his wife and Mey. He walked back through the prison doors. Soy wept with pity and sorrow for her husband.... Mey watched Sam until he disappeared from view, lost in thought.

"Let's go, Soy. Let's go home. Don't cry. There's no point in being sad. Three months isn't so long."

All the prisoners had gone. Mey took Soy back home in despair.

From the moment when Sam had gone to prison and been under the control of the guards, he had seen that it was no different from the visions of hell that old people talk about.

The guards led Sam to a different cell from the one he had been in yesterday. In this new cell, there were many prisoners crammed in together, sitting and lying down. The air was thick with a foul stench, like the stink of rotten fish mixed with the sweat of the prisoners. Every one of them had the dreadful face of someone who has been imprisoned many times, and never had any luck. The guard pushed Sam roughly into the cell, and then locked the door.

Sam saw the prisoners look him up and down with their mouths open wide. There was one prisoner who was dressed neatly and comfortably; he didn't look like a prisoner at all, more like a rich man. He looked Sam in the eyes, then cursed. "Damnit! The cell's crowded enough already, and they go and add this guy too! What are we going to do to get a place to sleep in here?"

All the prisoners turned and looked at the man speaking with an air of respect. His name was Huor. The judge had sentenced him to three months, too, for the crime of opening a gambling den. All the prisoners called him Brother Huor. Imprisonment for him meant only that he could not leave the confines of the prison, but nothing worse than that. Huor lived comfortably in the prison: he had a comfortable place to sleep, a mosquito net, a blanket, and delicious food to eat. The other prisoners in the cell always served him in any way he asked. The guards also held Huor in high esteem, and gave him special privileges in almost every regard. He slept in the cell, but had no need to work, and all this was because of the power of Huor's money....

One of the prisoners spoke up, trying to appear helpful. "Don't worry, Brother Huor, let him sleep at the end there, near the bucket." He pointed at the bucket that they used as a toilet. "If he dares to come close to you, Brother Huor, leave it to me, I'll kill him."

Sam saw that the prisoners in this cell had all truly become slaves to the power of money: the money of this Chinese man named Huor. There were going to be some serious disputes between Sam and these other prisoners, without a doubt.

Sam didn't bother with any of the others. He went and sat in down in a spot not so far from the area that belonged to this man named Huor. Immediately, Huor screamed at him: "Ah! Look at this! Go over there, go on! Don't come near to me, you hear? There's enough room over there for you to sleep."

Sam smiled, and replied in a gentle voice. "How can I sleep if I'm near the shit bucket like that?"

One of the prisoners, a very large and imposing man named Suos, who was a corporal, sprang to his feet and grabbed Sam by his left arm, pulling at his collar. "Are you a gangster, or what? Playing around, huh?" He spoke as if he had caused some problems of his own before this.

"No!" Sam replied, trying to control himself. "I'm not a gangster."

"So go on, then! Go over there. Don't come and bother Brother Huor."

"We can go wherever we want inside this cell," Sam answered with a smile. "After all, we're all prisoners, just the same."

"Ah! Talking like that, it seems like you're the only gangster here! So where are you from that you don't recognise me?"

Sam's face grew red with anger at being looked down on like this. He jumped up, leaned his back against the wall, and pointed his finger at Suos, who was the biggest of all the prisoners.

"You're a prisoner just like me! Can't you see? Don't let yourself be enslaved by this guy, my friend. Think of your fellow prisoners, come on! Look at me, I'm not a gangster. I'm just someone's son, just like you are. If you want to try something, then come on, I'm ready to fight you, my friend…."

Huor's whole body was shaking with anger. He screamed, "Come on, everyone! Why are you sparing this guy? A fancy guy like this, come on, let's get him! I'll give five cigarettes to all of you as a reward, and if there's any trouble, you can rely on me."

The promise of five cigarettes each made ten of the prisoners spring to their feet. They looked at Sam as if he was their most loathsome enemy.

One of the prisoners came right at Sam, but Sam dodged him. Bang! His fist crashed into the wall, and then Sam hit him square on the chin, making him fall over with loud thump. Eight or nine other prisoners, who hadn't yet joined the fight, surrounded Sam and began tearing at him. Huor stood and watched, propping his hands on his hips and looking very pleased with himself.

"Come on! Come on!" Huor urged them on like dogs. "Fight as hard as you can, this guy is tough!" The sound of thuds and punches filled the cell. Sam tried to stay strong, clenching his teeth and struggling to think of his old life. He thought it better to die fighting than to let these capitalist dogs savage him. He stood with his back to the wall, punching and kicking, and made two or three of the prisoners fall over.

But suddenly, one of the prisoners landed a kick with all his might directly on Sam's sternum. He fell flat onto the floor.

"Again! More!" Huor urged them on. Many more feet came and trampled on Sam's body.

Then two of the prison guards ran in, and shouted at the prisoners. "Stop! Stop! What the hell is this?"

The sound of the guards stopped their vicious torture. Sam moved his body, feebly, and the guards unlocked the door and came in to see what had happened. "What's going on?" asked one of the guards, who carried a thick whip in his right hand. "What's the trouble here?"

Huor answered immediately. "Who the hell is this guy? As soon as he arrived, he started kicking everyone, see! He even kicked me. If you don't believe me, ask anyone!"

"Yes, sir! That's how it was! This guy kicked all of us, and hard!" one of the prisoners answered, backing Huor's story. "When he came at me, I couldn't bear it, so I punched him right on the mouth. He tried to hit me back, and I stopped him, but he just kept punching. Come and look, sir. We've all got bruised and bloody faces because of him!"

"Yes, sir! That's how it was!" The other prisoners urged each other on, each adding a bit more to the story.

"Who the hell is this insolent guy, sir?"

The prison guard with the thick whip knocked Sam on the head with it. "Hey, you! Why'd you do that, huh?"

"Sir! It wasn't like they said!" Sam answered. He told the guard what had really happened. "Actually, they all attacked me when I arrived! When they saw that I wasn't afraid, they surrounded me and savaged me!"

"No! You can't believe him!" another of the guards said. "There was never any trouble with these guys before. Why all the fuss now?"

The guard with the thick whip lifted it up high, and beat Sam with it, utterly without mercy. The impact took his breath away; it almost killed him. Each blow hurt more than the one before, and the pain was indescribable. The whip drew blood from Sam's back; it took all his strength not to show his suffering.

Then the guard who had been whipping him suddenly stopped, and looked at Sam with a menacing expression. Sam took the chance to speak up.

"There is no justice in this world! You don't know the truth, but you punish me anyway, because of their version of the story. Can't you see, they're all lying, urging each other on, and all because of the power of money! A humble worker like me has no hope of getting justice. I have no choice but to bow my head and accept my fate."

"There's no point in complaining!" the guard growled. "Don't forget, even in court, the judge will believe their version of events. There's not one person here who will back you up; their stories all match!"

Sam's eyes filled with tears, and he began to cry. He cried in anger, in anger at himself for being born a poor man, for being born a peasant, and now for becoming a worker who everyone despised, looked down on, threatened and abused in every possible way....

Chapter 7

The Traffic Accident

Three months passed so slowly…. During his three months in the Kuk Thom prison, Sam suffered in unspeakable ways.

At last, the day of freedom arrived for Sam, the poor, unlucky worker. His hardship was finally at an end. The court had ruled that he was to be released on Tuesday morning.

The night before his release, Sam couldn't sleep at all. He was so excited to see the light outside the prison walls, and to be reunited with his poor wife.

At eight o'clock in the morning, the deputy prison chief called for Sam to report to his office. "Sam!" he said. "It's time for your release. You must do your best to do the right thing, now, Sam, and don't let me see you here again. I wish you all the best, I wish you success and happiness. Go on, Sam! Your lovely wife is waiting for you."

Sam raised his hands in a *sampeah* of thanks and respect to the deputy prison chief, and left his office feeling like a new man. He was so happy, to know the feeling of freedom once more.

A lovely woman's voice called out to him. Sam felt his hair stand on end. He turned to his right, and saw his poor, lovely wife running toward him, beaming with happiness. Sam and Soy greeted each other with tears of joy, mixed together with their tears of suffering.

"My dear! I've been waiting for you," Soy exclaimed. "I came with Mey. He's parked his *cyclo* over there."

Sam looked over and saw Mey standing by the *cyclo*, smiling and congratulating him for his freedom. He turned back to his wife. "Darling Soy. My punishment is over! Let's go, my dear. Let's get out of here, quick! I never want to see this place again." He took her by the hand, and led her over to where Mey was standing. The two friends shook hands and smiled to each other.

"Sam!" Mey said. "I'm so happy that you're free at last. You must start a new life now, Sam! And don't worry, I've found a *cyclo* to rent for you already, and the new owner is very kind."

Sam's eyes filled with tears. "Brother Mey! You're so kind to us. I'll never forget your kindness, in all my life."

"It's nothing," Mey answered. "Like I've told you before, we're friends, and that means that whenever either of us is suffering, the other will do anything we can to help. So go on! Hop on the *cyclo*, and I'll take you home."

"No, brother!" Sam answered. "You can ride in the *cyclo* with Soy, go on. Let me pedal it instead. I haven't driven a *cyclo* for three months, so let me pedal this time!"

Mey shook his head in refusal. "No! Don't, Sam. You're so excited by your freedom that you'd crash into someone for sure! And then we'd be in trouble all over again. Go on, let me pedal this time, it'll be easier." Sam grinned, and hopped onto the *cyclo* with his wife. Mey turned the vehicle around, and headed towards their home near the Wat Mahamontrey temple.

The next morning, Mey took Sam to meet the new *cyclo* owner, who was a widowed millionaire named Grandmother Kan. She was around fifty years old, and owned about thirty *cyclo*. When they arrived, she told them that regrettably all thirty had been rented out already. Sam felt defeated, but he sat down to talk awhile with Grandmother Kan. She asked him all about himself, and Sam told her everything, recounting every detail of his misfortune. Grandmother Kan felt very sorry for poor Sam.

"I really pity you and your wife," she said, truthfully. "Your hardships have been caused by wealthy people, I know, but please don't think that all wealthy people are nasty like that. We're not all the same. Some wealthy people really do understand about the life of poor people. I'm not trying to boast, but no matter what happens to me, I always feel sympathy for people who are poor. Mey knows it, too. I only charge very little rent for my *cyclo*—just twenty-five riels for one day and one night—and if it happens that you can't earn the money to come and pay the rental fee, I'll let you borrow from me too, and I never charge interest on the loan."

Sam raised his hands to *sampeah* to Grandmother Kan. He respected her sense of pity for the *cyclo* driving workers. "Madam! I humbly wish you the best of health and success in your every endeavour. If only other wealthy people could have compassion for the poor like you do, Madam, our lives would certainly be much easier."

"Well that settles it, then," Grandmother Kan said. "I'll help to find a *cyclo* for you to drive. Come back to see me in two or three days, and I guarantee I'll have a *cyclo* for you."

As Mey brought Sam home, they felt an indescribable joy. Sam felt sure he would be getting a *cyclo* soon, thanks to the kind millionaire's generosity.

* * *

At dusk on Friday, it was drizzling lightly. Sam rode his *cyclo* along Depot Boulevard, heading back home after bringing a passenger to the Eden Cinema.[9] A black Peugeot car drove up behind him, very fast. The driver was a woman, and a man sat next to her. She'd only recently learned how to drive from her boyfriend.

A Plymouth car was also coming very quickly toward Sam, from the front. The woman who was driving the Peugeot thought she would race against Sam's *cyclo*. Sam swerved to avoid the Plymouth that was heading towards him, just as it passed by. The inexperienced driver of the Peugeot was afraid she might crash into the Plymouth, so she jerked the steering wheel to the right, but the car veered too far off the road, and into the mud. She hit Sam's *cyclo* at full speed, and—crash!—the impact was like a stone smashing an eggshell.

The *cyclo* was overturned, and Sam went flying, landing flat on his face. The woman driving the Peugeot was terrified. She hit the brakes, but her boyfriend told her "Go! Quickly, go! Don't stop!"

The black Peugeot shot ahead like an arrow, and then turned away to the left. It sped off without any care for whether the driver of the *cyclo* was dead or alive, and no one saw the car's licence number, either.

Sam lay motionless. He had been knocked unconscious. The rain fell on him as the blood flowed from his head, his arms, and his legs. A crowd of people began to form, talking noisily but doing nothing to help him.

* * *

---

[9] The Eden Cinema was one of dozens of cinemas in central Phnom Penh during the time that the novel was written. It was located on Khemarak Phoumin Avenue (Street 130), near the Tonle Sap River, approximately three kilometres east of Depot Boulevard, which adjoins one of the city's large markets, Psar Depot market. A photograph from the US National Archives shows the Eden Cinema flourishing in 1961, when Suon Sorin's novel was published. See Roung Kon Project, "Location: 33 Former Cinemas in Phnom Penh," *Roung Kon Project: An Ongoing Archiving Online of Heritage Cinemas in Cambodia,* n.d., https://roungkonproject.wordpress.com/heritage-cinemas-in-phnom-penh-2/ [Accessed January 2019].

Mey and his family lived in a hot and stuffy hut, lit only by the pale light of a kerosene lamp. Mey, Mom and Soy were talking about Sam, who had taken his *cyclo* out in search of a fare in the early afternoon, and still not come back home. The three of them were worried that perhaps he'd been hit by a car, or caught by the police, or something.

Midnight passed…. The children in the neighbouring houses had all fallen asleep, and so had their parents; everything was silent. Rain drizzled quietly, and the air was cool, but they kept the door to the hut open. Mey, Mom and especially Soy couldn't stop staring out into the night. Every few minutes, Soy would go up to the doorway and look outside.

Sam never came home later than ten o'clock at night. He never went out socialising or drinking, and he never went to the movies or to the theatre, either. So of course, Mey, Mom and Soy couldn't help but be afraid.

Soy looked terrified, and she let out a long sigh. "I'm afraid Sam has been in an accident," she said.

"No! We don't know that yet," Mey insisted. "Sometimes passengers ask to travel a long distance, or they hire a *cyclo* to go around at all hours."

Soy sighed deeply again. "Don't remind me, Mey! These days, the city's not safe, you know!"

"Don't worry, Soy!" Mey said. "Sam's a good driver. He'd never let a car hit him. Don't get too agitated. Let's wait a bit longer, and if he's still not back, then I'll take my *cyclo* out and go look for him."

Hearing this, Soy looked relieved, but she was still worried. Her husband had never come home so late before.

One o'clock passed…. Sam still hadn't come back home. The three of them sat, huddled together in worry. "Mey! Please, take pity on me and go out to look for him, will you? I'm worried sick," Soy pleaded.

Before Mey could answer, Mom chimed in. "Yes, you should! It's very strange that he's not home yet. Go on, dear! And bring Soy to ride along in your *cyclo*, too!"

Mey looked at his wife. "But where should we go to look for him, huh?" he asked.

"Well, you should go to look in the hospital first!" Mom suggested. "If Sam has been in an accident, the police or anyone else involved will have brought him to the hospital. If you can't find him in the hospital, then you should go to look in the police station. Perhaps Sam has crashed into someone, or been involved in some kind of dispute, and been arrested."

Mey nodded his head. "You're right. Let's go!" Soy agreed.

Mey brought Soy to the Preah Ket Mealea Hospital, and parked his *cyclo* in front of the gate.[10] Soy hopped down from the *cyclo*, and Mey lifted his hands in a *sampeah* to greet the guard, who was sitting at his desk. "Excuse me, sir," Mey asked him. "Sir, have you seen a *cyclo* driver come in here, someone who had been in an accident?"

"Yes, we have!" the guard answered. "At seven-thirty, the police from the Chinese Hospital brought a *cyclo* driver here. He'd hit his head, and had some serious injuries."

Soy's heart sank. "Excuse me, sir," she asked the guard, in a pressing tone. "What was his name?"

The guard smiled, and said that he didn't know the man's name. "My job is just to guard the gate. But wait a moment, and I'll go to ask the nurse for you," he said. He went into the hospital for a moment, then rushed quickly back. "The patient's name was Sam! Is that right? Do you know him?"

"Yes!" Soy answered. "Yes, he's my husband!" She was in shock, hearing that her husband had been in an accident. She began to sob.

Mey asked the guard, in a panicked tone, "Sir! Can I please go inside to see him? Do you know how the patient is now?"

"I don't know how he is," the guard answered in a pitying voice, "but I heard them say it was very serious. Please, go ahead, go to the waiting room first, and ask to meet the doctor. Perhaps the doctor will give you permission to visit him." The guard pointed toward the entrance.

Mey followed the guard's directions, and brought Soy directly to the waiting room. A doctor and a nurse were standing by the doorway, and Mey and Soy both raised their hands and respectfully greeted the doctor with a *sampeah*.

"Your excellency!" Mey said to the doctor. "May I please visit Sam, sir?"

The doctor looked up, and thought for a moment. "Which Sam? The *cyclo* driver?"

"Yes, that's right!" Soy answered. "The guard told us that he'd been hit by a car, and was badly hurt!"

The doctor sighed deeply. "The patient is in great danger; he has very serious injuries. I can allow you to visit him for a few minutes, but please don't bother or disturb the patient, you hear? Come, he's in this ward." The doctor led Mey and Soy to Sam's hospital room. Soy sobbed, her tears flowing with pity for her husband. Soy thought that Sam must be the unluckiest man alive. He'd only been out of prison for a few days, and then a car had run into him!

---

[10] The Preah Ket Mealea Hospital, located in the city's north on France Street, was established during the colonial period.

Perhaps he would die tonight, if the injuries were too much for him to bear. After all, the doctor had warned her that Sam's condition was very dangerous.

The door to the ward was open, and the electric lights shone brightly inside. The doctor led Mey and Soy into Sam's room, and when they saw the bed to the left of the room, they stood in shock. Sam had been placed on a bed alone, and his body was covered in cuts and bruises, to which the doctor had carefully applied medicine. His head was wrapped all the way around in large bandages, and there was bright red blood on his neck. Both his arms were scratched and scraped, and his elbows were bleeding. Sam was fast asleep, and his breathing was shallow and irregular. His face was drained of colour, and his mouth was open slightly.

"Darling!" Soy screamed, her voice echoing through the room. She rushed toward Sam, but a nurse hurried over to stop her.

"Don't!" the nurse told her. "Don't touch him at all. The patient is in a great deal of pain. Let him sleep, he needs to save his strength."

Soy wept. Her heart felt like it would stop beating. She was overwhelmed with feelings of love mixed with pity.

"Your excellency!" Mey raised his hands in a *sampeah* as he addressed the doctor. "Where is the driver of the car that hit him, sir?"

The doctor looked tired. He yawned, and then he spoke very softly, as if he didn't want to answer Mey's question. "I don't know where they went. The police that brought the patient here said that the driver of the car had sped away, and disappeared. No one knows the car licence plate number." The doctor then turned toward Soy, and spoke to her with some welcome words of comfort. "Come, come, don't fret. I'll take care of him, to the best of my ability. Try not to worry too much, these things happen. Please, you head back home now, as the patient needs a lot of rest. His injuries are severe, and he's lost a lot of blood."

Soy looked intently at her husband's face, without blinking. Her tears were flowing, again.

"Let's go, Soy!" Mey whispered. "Let's go home. And don't speak too loudly, I'm afraid we'll wake Sam." They both bid farewell to the doctor with a *sampeah,* and turned to go home, filled with worry. As they left the room, Soy turned back to see her husband one more time, her heart heavy with sorrow.

* * *

The new month came to an end…. Sam had been in hospital for over a month. After the first week, his injuries began to heal well. Thanks to the expertise of the highly respected doctors at Preah Ket Mealea Hospital, Sam was almost himself again. When he was finally well, the doctor granted him permission to be discharged, and to return home.

The car that had hit Sam still could not be found. But Sam's injuries were not his fault, and he had been hurt through no action of his own. Not only that, but his *cyclo*, which was essential to his livelihood, had also been completely destroyed.

Sam resolved that he would no longer drive a *cyclo* to earn a living…. He decided to find another job, instead. Driving a *cyclo* didn't earn him enough money, and it left him utterly exhausted, every day drenching himself in sweat. It was not good for his health, and what's more, it was perilously dangerous. Cars in the city drove so fast, as if they were racing each other. No one drove at the legal speed limit, which was just thirty kilometres an hour.

There were many more victims of traffic accidents, suffering all kinds of injuries. A great deal of people lost their lives, too.

Chapter 8

The Foreign Capitalist

The more he thought about it, the more it seemed to Sam that his fate was improving. He had been searching for work for only a few days when he got a job as a worker, in a factory making soap. The owner of the factory was Chinese, and he employed more than twenty people.

It was as if Sam had begun a new life…. He had transformed from working as a *cyclo* driver to working in a factory making soap, and he earned a daily wage of just twenty-five riels, for ten hours of work.

The days passed, and turned into months…. Sam's hard work and diligence won him a pay rise, to thirty riels a day. After he'd been working there for two months, the supervisor, who was the son of the owner, began to trust and care for Sam. All of the other workers also liked Sam very much, and appreciated his kind temperament.

A person's luck can change suddenly… One day, the soap factory supervisor called Sam to join a private meeting. He said, "Corporal Kan has quit his position. So now I'm appointing you, Sam, to be the new corporal, and I'll increase your daily wage by another five riels, too, so that you'll earn thirty-five riels in a day.[11] I hope that you'll be responsible and always ensure that the coolies work in an orderly fashion."

Sam was absolutely delighted. "Sir!" he said. "I'll do my best to please you."

"Good, Sam!" the supervisor replied with a smile, and pointed to a small room that was within the factory compound. "Sam, you should come to stay in the room that Kan used to use. It's the room for the corporal. You can move in any day you like."

---

[11] Originally a military title and rank, a corporal was likely equivalent to a foreperson or manager.

Because he had to live in the soap factory, Sam moved out from staying with Mey and Mom. He brought his poor, pitiful wife to stay with him at the workplace, too. And from that day forth, Sam carried out his duties perfectly and tirelessly, with the hope that this job would bring him a bright and prosperous future.

* * *

The rainy season came and went. The weather became very cold. Sam had worked in the factory for eight months.

One afternoon, the owner, whose name was Seng Ly, came with a man to the factory to inspect the operations. As soon as they arrived, the owner saw that the workers were all working very hard, and in a good and orderly manner. Seng Ly told all the workers that the old supervisor, whose name was Seng An and who was the son of the owner, had travelled to Hong Kong to oversee the trade of their goods there. Now he was appointing his nephew, Seng Hong, to replace Seng An as supervisor.

After briefly inspecting the various operations, the owner got into his car and drove back to his house. That evening, shortly before it was time to stop work, Seng Hong, who behaved in a very superior and haughty way, spoke rudely and cruelly to the workers. To demonstrate how powerful he was, as a member of the capitalist class, he called Sam into his office and told him various things that he needed to change and improve about his work.

Sam didn't like this new supervisor at all. Seng Hong was a completely different person from Seng An.

"Sam!" the supervisor addressed him in a rude tone. "Starting from tomorrow, I need to get rid of ten Khmer coolies. You have to choose which ones should go and which ones should stay, and you have to tell them now that there's no need for them to come back to work tomorrow. I'll give them their final wage. And then I'll look for some Chinese and Vietnamese coolies instead, because Khmer coolies are so lazy and work so slowly. As for you, Sam, I'll keep you on as corporal."

Sam was shocked. The orders of his new supervisor were like a death sentence for him, because he knew what the life of a worker was like. Sam knew that the workers in this soap factory were all poor, living hand to mouth and drenching themselves in sweat to make just enough money to survive. They had wives and families; if they had to suddenly stop working without any warning, it was certain that they'd be in serious strife.

"I'm sorry, sir!" Sam begged Seng Hong. "The coolies are all very hard working, sir! Don't fire them, please take pity on them!"

Seng Hong glared at Sam with a look of displeasure. "No! It's impossible, Sam!" he said in a rude tone. "Khmer coolies are very lazy, they can't make a profit. I have to fire them. It'll be better to hire Chinese and Vietnamese coolies instead."

Sam felt a sudden sense of determination. He must protest, on behalf of his fellow workers, who were like family to him. He spoke up, again. "Sir! Please, take pity on us. These workers have all dedicated their lives to the job, and they've all worked here for a long time, too."

"Sam!" Seng Hong answered him angrily. "Don't you get it? We should be profiting much more than this. If we get Chinese and Vietnamese coolies instead, or at least replace half with them, the work won't be like it is now! Khmers are such lazybones! Actually, I'd really like to get all Chinese and Vietnamese coolies, but to do that would seem a bit over the top."

Sam reddened in anger…. He looked at this new boss, and felt overwhelmed with frustration. "Sir! Sir, you should have sympathy for the Khmer coolies. Not one of them is lazy, I tell you, and they all work much more than they get paid!"

Seng Hong pointed rudely at Sam's face and screamed at him. "Sam! You have no business making me listen to your reasoning! Get out of here! Hurry, get out of my office, and go tell those Khmer coolies that I'm firing half of them from tomorrow onwards! I'll pay them what we owe them. And watch it! Don't say anything more about it or I'll fire you too!"

Sam stood and spoke, no longer with any respect at all. "Even if you don't fire me, sir, I'll quit anyway! If you don't take pity on those coolies, then you're done for!"

"Get the hell out of here!" Seng Hong shouted at him. "You want to lead a rebellion of the coolies, do you, Sam?"

Sam gritted his teeth in fury, but tried to hold it in, and walked out of the office.

When he went to tell the Khmer coolies about Seng Hong's plan, panic broke out right away. Some of the younger and more immature workers screamed curses about Seng Hong and went about being destructive, but Sam tried to calm his worker comrades and keep them quiet. He promised them that he would do whatever he could to overturn the immoral action of the foreign capitalist.

* * *

It was half past twelve…. The sound of the bell rang through the factory, telling the workers that it was time to stop work. They gathered all together in the yard in front of the factory. The Khmer workers were all furious that half of them had been fired. Some of them wanted to go and start a fight about it, but Sam stopped them. "Don't, my friends, don't! We don't have to solve this by force." He roused them. "We are workers living hand to mouth, and we're always looked down on and mistreated. But we have to take care and behave ourselves, and keep quiet."

"No, Sam!" someone said. "It's too much to bear, brother!"

"Oh, come on, everyone! To be born poor is always like this," Sam answered. "The only morality is in serving the boss, make no mistake! It would take nothing for us to go to jail, without even having done anything wrong. They've got money, so we'll always lose to them." Then Sam returned to the office of the supervisor to ask for his wages.

Seng Hong stood near the window, smoking a cigarette and looking unhappy. The sound of the angry workers' curses made him very irritated. As soon as he saw Sam come into his office, Seng Hong shouted at him. "Sam, damn you! You've led the coolies into a rebellion. Well, it's nothing for me to have you thrown in prison right away."

"It's not like that, sir," Sam answered. "I'm the mediator, actually."

"There's something wrong with your head!" Seng Hong said angrily. "I'm chasing you and your stupid head out of here too, Sam! I don't need you anymore. You have until tomorrow morning to get out."

Seng Hong counted the money for Sam, and shoved it at him angrily. Sam left the office, and went back to the workers to distribute their wages. They were all firing questions at him, and Sam felt almost too pained to answer.

But he told them everything, the whole terrible story. The workers listened anxiously. They were all worried about their lives in the future, because the foreign capitalist had fired them without warning. Everyone was furious with Seng Hong, but they didn't know what to do about it.

Sam left the group of Khmer workers there, and walked solemnly back to his house on the north side of the main building. He'd carried out his duties as corporal well, and even though the capitalist had fired him, the workers would definitely not forget his kindness. And on top of everything else, Sam had to bring his pitiful wife Soy out from their house at the soap factory, to return to stay temporarily once again with their friends Mey and Mom.

Sam told Mey all about what had happened at the factory. "Brother Mey," he said, "I don't want to bother you, but I have nowhere else to go. I've come to ask you if I can stay with you, until I can go to find a house…."

"Of course, you're welcome, Sam!" Mey replied kindly. "Stay here, it's no bother. Until you've found a new job, you can share my *cyclo,* too: you ride it in the night, and I'll ride in the daytime, and we can split the rental fee between us."

And so Sam stayed with Mey and Mom again. He always thought, only a friend who is a worker can understand what it is to be a worker.

Chapter 9

The Deceitful Politicians

The days and months continued to pass by…. Sam kept on trying his best to find work. His efforts paid off, and this success absolutely delighted him. Sam took a job in another factory, as a worker. His life was always twisting and turning, as was his destiny. After two or three months of hard work, Sam was promoted to the position of corporal. He had won the affection of all the workers in the factory, and he worked hard to support them in getting just treatment from the owner. As a result, the owner, who previously had loved Sam, had now begun to loathe and despise him.

Finally, Sam was fired from his position in the factory, despite having done nothing wrong….

He took a job as a manual labourer at the wharfs, and once again he was promoted to corporal. His good work made him beloved by all the workers. Because of this, Sam was the object of hatred from the capitalists, because he always supported the workers in their disputes. The capitalists united against him, and once again Sam was fired from his position. But the workers who had been there with him always remembered his good deeds; they would never forget this.

Following this, Sam was jobless and stayed at home for almost a month. He returned to driving a *cyclo* again, but he drove only during the daytime, earning just enough money to survive from one day to the next. At night, Sam's friend Mey would drive the *cyclo* instead. The two of them were happy living together. They led a lowly and very simple existence, eating and sleeping whatever and whenever they could, as is the way for poor people.

Sam had an idea to raise the living standards of workers, and he began to make himself the object of affection of *cyclo* drivers, too. He hated the cruel-hearted capitalists who always exploited the Khmer workers and peasants, and worshipped maliciousness. Sam had become a very well-known man among the society of workers.

He began to form a secret labour union, but because of the ignorance and stupidity of the workers, they didn't ask for the formal permission of the government. Many workers joined, but the upper levels of society looked down on the union and were suspicious of it, because it was for the poorest of the workers, who were without any education. Sam was appointed as the leader of the union, but unlike in other unions, it wasn't a prestigious position, because neither the leader nor the union had any assets other than their physical strength for manual labour. No one cared about them at all.

But after a while, the union began to grow, attracting more and more members. All of a sudden, two or three deceitful politicians, who could see what the future held, came to join the union and began to interfere in its affairs, both by proposing their ideas, and also by providing some money, which was a powerful lure for winning over the hearts of the workers, who didn't know what was what.

These politicians were planning to win the affection and trust of the union members, and thus place the union under their control. They wanted the union to be useful for them in the coming election, in which the politicians were all standing as candidates. The politicians knew very well that all Khmer workers had been born as peasants; they came to work in the city only when they weren't busy with ploughing in the countryside, and working in the rice fields and farms. The politicians had come to make connections among the workers, in order to make it easier for themselves when it came to the election, when they would need to rely on the workers to support them.

"Sam! Please, brother, have some compassion and help me, won't you?" One of the politicians spoke to Sam, in a manner that was very gentle and proper. "I've volunteered to stand as a candidate in the election. If you will help me, I hope that I can win, and if I'm elected, then please know that you'll have nothing to worry about. I'll do everything in my power to help the workers. I'll appeal to the government to lift the status and improve the living conditions of the workers, such as calling for *cyclo* drivers to have cheaper rental fees, and for the government to assist workers with obtaining housing, electricity, running water, and so on."

And in the end, the politicians did receive Sam's full support in the general election, and the support of the workers, and they won and were elected to the Senate, as they had wanted. But after that, the politicians stopped coming to the union to check on the well-being of the workers. The success and prosperity of the politicians was surely born from the support of the workers, but now, they had forgotten all of their promises. From then on, whenever the workers met them somewhere, the politicians would pretend that they didn't recognise them. Sam saw clearly for himself that workers are stupid and ignorant people, who could be easily tricked and deceived by politicians. He swore to himself that, from this day forward, he would never again allow the politicians to use and exploit him. He had always taken care of the politicians! But they always went back to their old ways, as politicians, see!

* * *

Along the streets of the capital, which were dusty and filled with many kinds of vehicles, Sam pedalled his *cyclo* under the heat of the hot sun, in search of a passenger. His was the kind of job that required a person to be drenched in sweat. It was an honest job, but it also made many in the upper classes look at him suspiciously.

Once again, the days and months passed by. Whatever comes to pass, it only comes to pass once, and only for but an instant; whatever happens in life is no different from a pleasant dream, that floats away in the moment when we wake, and disappears. Life's events cause suffering and fear for those who encounter them, and nothing more.

The lowly labour union that Sam was in charge of existed for just half a year, because it received no support at all from anyone other than the workers. In the end, it dissolved and disappeared, and the capitalists laughed and made fun.

A *cyclo* was still a *cyclo,* just the same…. And the workers who worked in the morning in order to eat in the evening, with nothing to depend on but their own strength, were still workers just the same.

The sound echoed through all the streets of the capital; the people sitting on the driver's seat of every *cyclo* were workers, who lived hand to mouth, doing exhausting work and drenching themselves in sweat. They did honest work, but they were looked down on by wealthy and important people.

In some restaurants, if ever a *cyclo* driver entered and sat down to eat, people would glare at him out of the corner of their eyes, showing their disrespect; others were so mistrustful and uneasy they would stand up and hurry away. Most workers would encounter this upsetting situation almost every day.

And what's more, the Chinese and Vietnamese still dared to pay "tea money" bribes to the landlords, too.[12] Sam and his friends had to separate and

---

[12] "Tea money" refers to an informal bribe, usually small, which is commonly understood as a necessary fee to facilitate a transaction.

find new places to live. Sam was out of money, and his worker friends allowed him to stay with them again, like before….

Sam and his pitiful wife Soy went to rent a small hut far from the city, on some vacant land that a capitalist had grabbed in order to sell in the future. The capitalist had built this tiny hut to secure the land. If he'd asked anyone with status higher than Sam's to stay in that tiny hut and guard the land, no one would agree. But Sam still earned a living by driving a *cyclo* like before. It was just enough to get by, but not enough to save any money, because there were some days when he earned almost nothing at all.

Some workers couldn't endure a life without any options. Some came to regard terrible things as being good, and they turned away from making an honest living, to follow the path of evil instead.

Chapter 10

City Gangsters

The month of March passed by. The trajectory of Sam's life was still shrouded in darkness, like always. His status had not improved at all. No matter what happened, Sam's situation was still the same as before, and his physical health continued to deteriorate, since he had no time to rest and the food he ate was lacking in nutritional value.

These days, Sam could no longer drive a *cyclo* for a full day like he did before, because his limbs often ached from exhaustion. It was more and more difficult for him to make a living, but he could still be considered to have good fortune, since he was able to rent a *cyclo* to drive.

Now, Sam had a heavy responsibility: Soy was ready to give birth to their child. Sam didn't have enough money to buy the things they needed, or medications. So he had to grit his teeth and go to drive his *cyclo* to try to make some money, for perhaps two or three hours, and then bring it home to keep in case of emergencies.

That day, from dawn until dusk Sam had not left the house to drive his *cyclo* at all, because he felt hot and then shivery, as if he was on the verge of having a fever.

"My dear," Soy said to him. "If you're not feeling well, please relax a little, or you might get even more sick."

"Do we have any money left?" Sam asked her.

"Yes! We still have forty riels."

"Forty riels!" Sam sighed deeply. "But we've run out of rice and charcoal for cooking, haven't we?"

"Don't worry!" Soy said, to comfort her husband. "We still have some rice left, and we can gather a bit of charcoal from here and there to use in the meantime. Please rest for a day, my dear, and wait until tomorrow to go to earn some money. As for the rental fee for the *cyclo*, we can ask the owner for a loan for two or three days."

"Hmm," Sam replied tensely. "I don't know when things will get easier for us, my dear."

"Don't worry about it too much! If we try hard to make an honest living like this, surely the day will come when the gods will help us."

"Unless the gods have mercy on us, we will be damned, my dear! We haven't yet bought any of the things we need for our baby, and if you go into labour today or tomorrow, I don't know where you'll give birth, as we don't have any money…."

Soy gazed sympathetically at her husband, and said, "I'll give birth in the hospital, darling! I can take a bed in the area for homeless people. So if ever I'm feeling unwell, you can take me to hospital. Once we have the baby, after I've come back home from the hospital you can go to buy the things we need, for sure. So lie down and rest, my dear, I'll go and cook some rice." Soy went to tend to the stove, which they kept in the same room that they slept in.

Sam slowly stretched himself out on an old mat on the floor, resting his head on his arm in place of a pillow…. He thought of the hardships of making a living. But he didn't know of any other *cyclo* driver who had enjoyed good fortune like him, to have stopped driving a *cyclo* and go to do another, better job instead.

Night began to fall…. The moon in the east shone brightly.

After bathing and eating, Sam felt a little better, and had enough energy to go to earn some money on the *cyclo*.

He told his wife that he would go out for a while. Soy didn't want him to go, but Sam promised that he'd come back home within two to three hours at the most, so she agreed to let him leave.

After leaving their tiny hut, which was like a rat's nest, Sam drove his *cyclo* quickly along the road. Finally when he reached the Koun Kat Bridge, he met two passengers, both middle-aged men who had just come out from a Chinese shophouse.[13] The two men raised their hands to hail the *cyclo*, and then when they were riding they used their hands to signal to Sam which direction they wanted him to drive. When the *cyclo* had travelled quite far from where they began, one of the men said, "We're just going for a drive for fun," indicating that they did not have a final destination in mind.

---

[13] A shophouse is a ubiquitous architectural type found across much of Southeast Asia, and beyond. It combines a private dwelling, typically for a family unit, with a flexible space often used for various kinds of business.

Hearing them say this, Sam was delighted, as he realised that he would make at the very least twenty riels from this trip, since the men were just driving around to relax.

The *cyclo* turned this way and that, travelling along various streets, and paused to wait at a few places, too. Finally, Sam pedalled the *cyclo* to Wat Phnom, as instructed by the passengers.[14] The two men were whispering to each other, but Sam didn't pay attention to what they were saying. After a short while, the *cyclo* arrived at the east side of Wat Phnom, and the men asked to stop there.

Sam stopped the *cyclo* as instructed; he felt tired. In that very instant, one of the men suddenly jumped out from the *cyclo*, and pulled out a dagger. The other passenger got down out of the *cyclo*, too.

"Don't scream! Do you have any money? Quickly, give it to us!"

It was hopeless! Sam had no energy, and there were no police around! His only hope was to raise his hands in a respectful *sampeah* gesture, and plead with them. He begged: "I have no money, sir! I had only just left my house when I met you."

"Don't try to resist! Give it to us, quick, quick!" one of the men said menacingly.

"I have no money at all, sir! If you don't believe me, sir, you can go ahead and check!"

The two men checked in the pockets of Sam's shirt and his trousers, and in his *cyclo*. When they saw that he had no money at all, not even a cent, one of the men kicked Sam, and swore at him. "You damned idiot! I thought you had some money!"

Then the two thieves ran off together.

It was eleven o'clock at night already…. Sam, this unfortunate and pitiable *cyclo* driver, pedalled back home with a feeling of hopelessness.

He stopped the *cyclo* in front of the hut. The door was still open. Sam looked in, and saw his wife lying down. The light of the oil lamp burned faintly, and Sam called out to her from afar. Hearing him, Soy sat up.

"Soy! Today I was so unlucky, my dear!" Sam told his wife as he came in to her. "Two gangsters tried to rob me, but I hadn't earned any money at all yet." He explained everything that had happened, while his wife listened.

---

[14] Located at the northern edge of the historical city, Wat Phnom is a hill topped by a Buddhist pagoda and several stupas. According to legend, Wat Phnom was first established in the 14th century CE by an old woman named Penh. The city is named after the site.

"Darling!" Soy said, with tears of pity for her husband. "I'm not sure, but I think perhaps I will give birth tonight."

Sam's eyes opened wide, and he asked, "How do you know?"

"Because my belly is so sore, and it's getting worse and worse. It's come two or three times now, and it's not like a normal belly ache."

Sam rubbed his wife's shoulders comfortingly, and then said in a terrified voice, "My dear! I don't have enough money for you to give birth in a hospital that charges fees. It looks like you will need to give birth in a government hospital, in the place for homeless people…."

"Don't worry! Anywhere is fine, as long as the birth goes smoothly."

The husband and wife sat talking together under the roof of their silent hut, with the oil lamp burning faintly. They were both terribly afraid and suffering. It was as if their lives were floating on the ocean, without any land in sight, in the middle of a typhoon.

Chapter 11

Soy Dies with No One to Take Care of Her

It was the middle of the night.... Around half past two o'clock in the morning.

Soy's belly was growing more and more painful, and she almost couldn't bear it any more. She realised that the time had definitely come for her to give birth. She tried to shake her husband awake, and make him get up.

"Hey, my dear! I'm in a lot of pain!" she told her husband. "If this is how it's going to be, then it looks like I might die, for sure. Only now do I realise how my own mother suffered, like I am, too! Oh! Why is it so painful, my dear?"

Sam woke from his sleep in a daze, and tried to comfort his wife by hugging her and holding her in his arms. "Try to bear it a little longer, darling!" Sam said to comfort his wife. "I will go to call San, and ask him to drive us to the hospital in his *cyclo.*"

Soy shook her head. "No, dear. It looks like I can't go to the hospital. I'm in so much pain, I won't be able to stand riding in a *cyclo* to the hospital. I think I'm going to die!"

"In that case, what should we do?"

"You should go to ask Doctor Norea to come and save my life."[15]

"Then bear with it just a little longer, okay? I will go to get the doctor."

Sam hurriedly pedalled his *cyclo* away from the hut, until he reached a big house on the main road. Then he slowed down, to read the sign.

---

[15] Norea, a common name, is also a word connoting a "good man". This is one of many instances of Sorin's use of ironic names for characters.

Sam stopped his *cyclo* directly in front of the gate in the wall that surrounded the big, concrete house. It was the home of Doctor Norea, who was renowned for his ability to cure disease.

Sam pressed the electric doorbell. He stood and waited impatiently for a while, and then someone walked over from the house and opened the gate, calling out: "Who's there?"

Sam answered immediately, in a respectful tone. "I've come to ask the doctor to come and attend to my wife, who is giving birth."

The latch of the gate opened slowly. The person who had come to open the gate was the doctor's servant. He glanced at Sam, not really looking at him. The electric light on top of the gate was as bright as thirty-five candles, so the servant could see that Sam was the *cyclo* driver who rented the hut that was all the way along the alleyway below. He felt deep empathy and pity as he looked at Sam's face.

"It looks like you're out of luck, brother!" the servant said to him. "If I go in and wake the doctor, he'll be angry at me for sure. There's no hope that he'll go to attend to your wife. It's not easy at night like this. Even if the patient was an important or wealthy person, maybe the doctor would go, but I still wouldn't dare to say for sure."

Sam took a long, deep breath. He raised his hands in a polite and respectful *sampeah* to the doctor's servant, and then pleaded him with him, in pitiful words. "Please, kindly take a chance and go in to wake the doctor. Perhaps he'll agree to go. Please, take pity on me, won't you?"

The doctor's servant seemed to be feeling very unsure and uncomfortable.

"I really pity you, my brother, but … he'll surely just curse and scold me." He hesitated for a moment, then he continued: "But yes of course, brother! We are both poor people, just the same. I'll take a chance, and go to wake the doctor, and see how it goes. Come on! Come inside, brother; you'll need to really plead with him, you hear? Perhaps he'll take pity and go with you…."

Sam followed the servant, and walked into the property. He stood and waited at the bottom of the stairs.

The doctor's servant went upstairs into the house. Instantly, the electric lights on the balcony came on. A big and fat middle-aged gentleman, wearing pyjamas, walked out of the central room. This was Doctor Norea, who was famous throughout the capital.

The servant had just woken the doctor, and informed him that there was someone asking him to go to see his wife who was giving birth. The doctor had misunderstood, thinking that it was his neighbour from nearby, and had hurried out from his bedroom to ask about her condition.

But when he saw Sam, the doctor immediately scowled in anger. Sam kneeled down in genuflection, and lifted his hands in a *sampeah* gesture to the doctor, who was standing on the stairs.

"Please, your excellency, please take pity on this impoverished being, won't you? My wife is giving birth and in great pain, and I have come to ask your excellency to please come to see to her."

"Tsk tsk," the doctor clicked his tongue in displeasure, and then frowned. He refused to say anything to Sam, other than to glare at him doubtfully out of the corner of his eyes. Then he turned to address his servant.

"Damn it, Suos! You're very brave, to have dared to wake me while I was sleeping peacefully! I thought that someone from the big hospital had come for me. If I knew that this was the situation, I wouldn't have come! Oh, damn it, Suos! You are so stupid, that's for sure!"

Sam bowed his head down, and once again lifted his hands in a *sampeah* to the doctor. With a trembling voice, again he pleaded with him.

"If your excellency won't please agree to come and rescue us, my wife's life will surely end while she is in labour, sir!"

"No!" the doctor answered angrily. "I take no responsibility if your wife lives or dies. Get out of here."

"Please, your excellency, please have mercy, sir."

"Don't come and talk to me about mercy and cruelty! I don't need mercy. So go on, take her to the big hospital. You can only bring me to see her if you pay me, and it has to be at least 1,000 riels, too. My studies were not cheap; did you ever give me anything to help with my studies, hmm? You keep asking me to pity you, but how can I? Go on, get out of here, and take her to the big hospital."

When he had finished talking, Doctor Norea went back upstairs into the house. Sam gritted his teeth, wanting nothing but to scream abuse, to cry out that poor people were no different from wild beasts. But Sam thought of his wife, who was lying in pain; if he yelled at the doctor, perhaps there would be trouble. He rushed out from the doctor's property.

Feeling hopeless, Sam pedalled his *cyclo* back to the hut. Just before reaching home, he heard by the sound of Soy's moaning that her pain had become more acute.

Sam stopped the *cyclo* in front of the hut. In the light of the oil lamp, he saw his friend San, the worker who lived in a neighbouring house, sitting and watching over Soy with a terribly worried look on his face.

Sam's heart burned with pity for his wife. He rushed in and sat next to her, and when Soy opened her eyes and saw her husband, it seemed as though a little of her energy returned.

"Oh!" she screamed in pain. "Did you ask Doctor Norea to come, my dear?"

Sam caressed her head comfortingly. "Oh, my darling! I'm at the end of my wits," he told his wife. "The doctor refused to come. He said that if I gave him 1,000 riels, then he would come. Huh! What kind of doctor needs to be offered money like a god?"

When he had finished speaking, Sam turned to San. "San! Take pity on us, and don't go back home yet, eh? We have no one but you. Take pity and stay with us!"

"Don't worry, Sam," San said, nodding his head in agreement. "I'll stay and help you until your wife has given birth. Don't worry, we always help each other."

Tears fell from Sam's eyes: tears of pity and despair. At that moment, an old lady appeared at the door of the hut. She was thin and hunched, and was also one of Sam's neighbours. Her name was Pong, and she lived with her nephew, who was a manual labourer at the docks.

Sam and San turned to look at Pong. "Oh, is that you, Grandmother Pong?" Sam called to her. "Please come in."

Pong walked into the house, and sat down next to Soy, who was lying and moaning. "What's happening, my child?" Pong asked. "Why don't you take her to the hospital?"

"Soy says she can't ride on a *cyclo*," Sam replied. "Because her belly is in so much pain, and the hospital is far. Perhaps we can't make it."

"Oh!" Pong said. "In that case, what can we do? I'm no expert in this, either, but I can help you a little. Perhaps you should go to ask a doctor to come, no?"

"Yes, Grandmother Pong!" Sam answered sadly. "But he refused to come. And he said he would charge at least 1,000 riels, too."

"Hmm!" Pong said. "We live hand to mouth! Where can we find 1,000 riels? Sam! It looks like Soy is giving birth now. You need to light a fire, and boil some water for me. I'll do everything I can to help you, Sam! To be born poor is always so difficult, like this."

Sam gritted his teeth. He looked at his beloved wife, and was filled with pity.

"Grandmother!" He turned to Pong. "A doctor should do everything he can to help his brothers and sisters, and not be choosy about whether they are rich or poor, or of what nationality or religion. But now I know that there are some doctors who worship money like it's a god, and that there are very few doctors who will do everything they can to help their brothers and sisters."

"That's right, Sam! Don't talk too much," San interrupted. "Let's just worry about our own problems, come on. I'll light the fire and boil the water for you. If there's anything I can help with, just ask me. We're both workers, and we must help each other in turn. If we can't help with money, then we can help by doing things for each other."

"Thank you very much, San, for taking pity on us."

San said nothing in reply, but went to look for the stove.

For a moment, all was still. Soy sat and lay down in turns; her face was ghostly pale, and she was drenched in sweat. Grandmother Pong started to organise and delegate tasks in the manner of a traditional midwife.

Soy's pain would come and go. At one moment, when she was in more pain than before, she rubbed herself on the belly, and cried out loudly, in a pitiful voice.

Sam rushed back and forth, here and there, in a fearful panic. Finally, he slid over to sit with his wife, and lay her down in his arms, while speaking to her in a comforting voice. "Soy, darling! Please try to hold on a little longer. Soon the pain will go, my dear!"

Soy hugged her husband tightly, shuddering from the sharpness of the pain. After inspecting her belly, Grandmother Pong sighed deeply. She lifted her head, to look up at Sam's face. "The baby is coming out breach," she said. "Oh! Where did San go?"

San called out from the kitchen, and came to Pong who was sobbing. "Help drive me over to the Chinese hospital," she said to him. "I'll go to ask Grandmother Pos to come and help as the midwife. I can't do it. Now that the baby is coming out breach, only Grandmother Pos can help. Let's go, quickly, and hurry back. Letting her suffer like this is not easy."

Sam lifted his hands in a *sampeah* to Pong, and spoke in a trembling voice. "Thank you very much, Grandmother. Please take pity and have compassion for us. I have no one to depend on, other than you, Grandmother."

Pong stood up hurriedly, and led San out from Sam's hut. The *cyclo* headed out of the alleyway, toward the main road. Soy's pain was intense. Sam could do nothing to help his wife, other than to sit and hug her. "My darling Soy," he said, with tears in his eyes. "This is only happening because you are my wife. If not for that, you wouldn't be suffering like this. Try to be patient, my dear! Soon, Grandmother Pong will be back."

Soy took her husband's hands and squeezed them tightly, then cried out in pain. "Oh, my dear! I'm dying! Oh, the gods and the angels, please may they come to save the life of my child!"

* * *

Thirty minutes had passed…. San was trying to pedal the *cyclo* as quickly as he could, along the middle of the dark and silent road. Grandmother Pong sat on the *cyclo* with another old woman, who was a traditional midwife. Pong was terribly anxious and impatient.

When she had arrived at the house of Grandmother Pos, Grandmother Pong knocked on the door and called out in a friendly voice.

Grandmother Pos hurried to prepare herself a basket of betel, and then immediately came out of the house and climbed up to ride off in the *cyclo* with Grandmother Pong.[16] She was very happy to go help, and didn't ask for any payment.

The *cyclo* turned into the alleyway that led to Sam's hut, and San was still trying his hardest to pedal quickly. He didn't slow down until the moment he reached the hut, because he was so worried about Soy's condition.

San hopped down from the *cyclo*, and rushed straight into the hut. He instantly turned white with fear. What San saw made him shake and tremble. Soy was lying on the floor, perfectly straight, and there was an old blanket covering her almost from head to toe. Sam was resting his head on the blanket and weeping. San realised that Soy had left this world, and that she would never come back.

In that moment, Grandmother Pong had led Grandmother Pos into the hut behind San, and they too cried out when they saw Soy's body lying straight under the blanket, her soul had already departed.

"Oh, Buddha! What a pity, what suffering! Oh!" Grandmother Pong murmured in prayer, her face solemn as she turned to look at her beloved Grandmother Pos. "We came too late," she said. "She's dead."

Grandmother Pos stood for a moment, her face ghostly pale, and then she softly spoke in a trembling voice. "Oh! Buddha, oh! Please allow her soul to be born into happiness! We had come to try to save her, but we were too late to be of any help. She had already breathed her last, because she couldn't give birth to her child. If I had arrived just half an hour earlier, perhaps she wouldn't have died. In fact, Grandmother Pong, you should have come for me as soon as she began to suffer! Oh!"

Grandmother Pong led Pos over to sit by the body…. Sam lifted his head and looked at the two old women. His face was stained with tears, his hair was a mess, and his eyes were red with sorrow. In that moment, it was like Sam was unconscious, in a daze.

---

[16] Betel leaf, usually combined with areca nut or tobacco, is commonly consumed in much of Southeast Asia.

"Greetings, Grandmother!" he said tearfully, and lifted his hands in a *sampeah*. "Soy has died and left me! She died in my arms. I have never been so afraid as I was when she died. Thank you so much, Grandmother, for coming to help. Even though you didn't come in time, still you came to help, you came to save your brothers and sisters. We are all human, just the same."

Grandmother Pos was motionless, and said nothing. She sat and gazed solemnly at the body. San went and sat next to Sam and stroked his back gently. In a comforting voice, he said, "Sam! No matter what we do, death is normal, and it's the fate of all people on earth! This was your wife's fate, Sam. Don't be too sad. You must remember that no one can escape from death, eh, Sam…."

"San! I don't believe that this death was her fate!" Sam replied with tears in his eyes. "My wife died because no doctor or midwife came to help. If there was a doctor or a midwife here, then I would have a child, who could bring me joy and happiness, San…."

"But whatever the case, your wife has already died," San said, to comfort Sam. "We shouldn't think any more about the doctor or the midwife. Nothing will make her live again, you see, Sam! We should think about arranging the funeral."

"That's right, Sam!" Grandmother Pong interrupted to say. "Come on, don't think too much. We should plan Soy's funeral, come on. I'll do everything I can to help you."

"My wife's funeral!" Sam cried out in anguish. "Oh! Grandmother, what can I do? I have no money at all. It's hopeless, Grandmother. I am such an unlucky person. I have only thirty riels left; you can imagine my hardship. I can't plan my wife's funeral with that, Grandmother."

Grandmother Pos took a deep breath. She reached into her shirt pocket, and then moved close to Sam, and passed him two ten-riel notes. "Sam!" she said. "Please allow me the merit of giving you this twenty riels, my child. I am also so poor! We both work in the morning to eat in the evening, but I am delighted to help another poor person, you see! I will say goodbye now, and go back home, Sam."

Sam felt an incomparable gladness in his heart. He thought to himself, Grandmother Pos is poor, she is a traditional midwife, but she is delighted to help to save me with her sense of humanity. And when she was too late to save my wife, she was willing to offer me twenty riels to help with the funeral. And twenty riels for her is a great deal.

Sam lifted his hands in a *sampeah* gesture to Grandmother Pos, and respectfully accepted the twenty riels.

"Grandmother! I thank you very much," Sam said in a trembling voice. Then he turned to look at San. "San! You see how very different Grandmother Pos is from that Doctor Norea? Oh, San! It is only the poor who can understand the poor. Please, will you help to bring Grandmother Pos back to her house, eh, San?"

"Ah, of course, Sam!" San nodded in agreement. "It's no trouble, I'll bring her home. If there's anything else that I can do for you, Sam, please don't be afraid to tell me. I'll do everything in my power to help you, no matter how difficult. I'll help you with the funeral of your wife, so that it can go smoothly. When we're poor, we do everything to help each other, eh, Sam."

Sam smiled through his tears, pleased by San's words. He watched as San led Grandmother Pos out of the hut.

Grandmother Pong had gathered some joss sticks, and lit them at the head of Soy's body. She arranged the things in the hut to be neat and tidy. As for Sam, he had no energy to help at all. He just sat with his head bowed against his knees and wept sorrowfully with pity for the corpse of his wife.

Sam, the pitiful and unlucky worker, had his wife die and leave him, because she could not give birth to her child without any assistance from any doctor or midwife…. And not only that, but the *cyclo* that is the most important thing for Sam's livelihood was also taken back by its owner, because he had no money to pay the rental fee. Sam's life was in a terrible crisis. Sam had done everything he could. He was ready to follow his wife. He was able to prepare Soy's funeral quietly, because of the help from his worker friends, who each offered a little money.

Chapter 12

The Ungrateful Politicians

The twists and turns, changes and instabilities in people's lives always become like normal, and this is true of Sam's life, too....

Now, Sam was unemployed again. Every single day, he strived diligently to find a job. He tried especially hard to find a *cyclo* to rent, but all the *cyclo* owners demanded a deposit of at least 150 riels.

Sam felt very fondly toward Mey and Mom, because during Soy's funeral, they had both given a lot of money to help with the ceremony, and also because there had been so many times when Mey and Mom had rescued Sam when he'd fallen on hard times. He realised that there was no one at all who could support him like these two had done.

One day, Sam walked despairingly over to Mey and Mom's house. When he arrived, he saw that Mey was unwell, lying down and looking sick, pale and drawn. Both his knees were abnormally swollen, because they had retained fluid from pedalling the *cyclo* too much.

"Sam!" he called out, softly. "I've been sick almost half a month already, and my *cyclo* has been taken back by its owner, too. It's really difficult for me lately. My wife has to make cakes to sell, in order to make some money. How about you, Sam? Have you found a *cyclo* to rent?"

Seeing Mey sick like this melted away any intention of Sam's to come and ask him for a favour.

"Oh, brother Mey! I had no idea that you were sick. I haven't found a *cyclo* yet, but I've been looking! Do we know anyone who would be able to share their *cyclo* for me to drive? I could borrow it either during the daytime, or at night."

"No, Sam! I can't seem to think of anyone." Mey struggled to sit up, and spoke slowly. "Lately, we *cyclo* drivers have really struggled to make any money. Everybody tries to work day and night."

Sam asked about Mey's symptoms and condition, and then turned back to the subject of the *cyclo* again. "Brother Mey! I would do some other job, but that's impossible, too, because I don't know how to do anything whatsoever. If I can't find a *cyclo*, it looks like I might die of starvation."

"If that's how it is, then you can come to stay with me in the meantime, Sam." Mey looked at Sam, and spoke with empathy. "I trust you completely."

"No! I can't do that, brother." As he spoke, Sam tried to smile through his despair. "I bother you so much, there is no one as good as you. I really thank you, brother. So let's just see where fate takes me. If I die, then let me die. If I do nothing but bother you, when you're already sick like this, then I'll just make it more difficult for you."

"No, don't think like that, Sam!" Mey shook his head, and sounded exhausted as he spoke. "We are poor people, so it's always difficult for us, but we have to help each other when we can." Mey sighed deeply. "Oh! Of course! Sam, you should go to see Mr Yeng Sak. Perhaps he'll have a way to help you. Nowadays, he's very rich! He owns thirty or forty *cyclo*, and I'm sure he'd still remember you, because when he stood as a candidate in the election, you helped him to win the support of us workers. You really helped him a lot, I could almost say that Mr Yeng is an elected representative only because of your support, eh, Sam!"

"Will he still recognise me, Mey?" Sam asked. "I've heard people saying that Mr Yeng Sak is now very highly ranking, and doesn't really let anyone meet him or bother him any more."

"But I think maybe he won't have forgotten your kindness, Sam," Mey answered. "Go to visit him and see. Ask to rent one of his *cyclo* to drive; his *cyclo* are all new, and I think we won't take a deposit from you, because we all need to remember each other's kindnesses sometimes, don't you think, Sam? I still haven't forgotten that Mr Yeng promised to you that he would represent poor people, as a way to get you to help him with all your energy. He said he'd help to improve the living conditions of poor people, and he wouldn't forget your kindness, until the day he dies…."

Sam sat and thought for a moment before he answered. "If that's the case, I'll take a chance and go to visit him, and see how it goes. If I'm lucky, perhaps he'll take pity on me and let me rent his *cyclo*."

Sam sat and talked with Mey for about half an hour, before he went back. He told Mey that if he was able to find a *cyclo* to rent, he'd come back to tell him.

That afternoon, Sam arrived at the house of the representative of the poor, Mr Yeng, who now had a very high position, and a great deal of influence in governmental affairs. It was a concrete house, very large and modern, and on a big property. On the north side of the house, there was an enormous shed for *cyclo*. Mr Yeng's status had transformed in the space of just one year: he'd gone from being at the bottom, to being at the top. Before he had become a people's representative, Mr Yeng had only a small, thatched house, and wore only old clothes. Wherever he went, he would always ride an old bicycle. But fate had permitted Mr Yeng to very quickly become well-established as a rich man. He had money to buy property, and to buy thirty or forty *cyclo* for renting out. He had also bought two beautiful American cars. No one would ever know where his abundant wealth had come from.

After Sam had walked onto the walled property, and stood in front of the house, he caught sight of several young women frolicking together upstairs in the house. In front of the shed for *cyclo*, he saw two repairmen who were mending some of the vehicles.

Sam had been standing and watching all this for almost ten minutes, before he saw a slightly older man coming down from the house. Sam walked over to him, and raised his hands in a *sampeah* gesture. "Excuse me, sir!" he asked. "Is Mr Yeng in?"

"Yes, he's here!" the servant answered brusquely. Without pause, he asked Sam, "What business do you have with him?"

Sam thought that if he told this man the truth—that he had come to ask Mr Yeng for help—then the man would most likely refuse, by making some excuse like that Sir was not available to receive visitors. So, he decided to lie to the man. "Sir has asked for me to come to meet him," Sam said.

"In that case, please wait a moment, I'll go to inform him that you're here."

The man went back upstairs, and disappeared into the house. After a moment, a middle-aged man walked out from the house. He wore white trousers, a white silk button-down shirt, and a necktie. This gentleman was Mr Yeng, the people's representative and a member of the Senate. When the servant had gone in to inform him that there was a man here asking to meet him, because he'd asked the man to come, Mr Yeng couldn't recall anyone at all whom he'd invited to meet him. He figured that perhaps it was a *cyclo* driver who'd come to pay to him the deposit for a vehicle.

When he saw Sam's face, Mr Yeng was startled. He still remembered him as the former head of the labour union, a man who had been important in helping to vocally publicise for the benefit of Mr Yeng, without receiving anything whatsoever in repayment.

Now, Mr Yeng's promises had dissolved into air, and were of no use at all to the workers. Their only value was to Mr Yeng, who had tricked and cheated the poor into believing in him. Immediately, he knew for sure that Sam had come to ask for a favour. He pretended not to recognise him, and he asked: "What business do you have here, my friend?"

"Your excellency!" Sam said, as he raised his hands in a *sampeah*. "Have you forgotten me already, sir?"

Mr Yeng frowned, and pretended to be trying to remember. "Ah! I seem to have forgotten. Have we met before?"

Sam smiled bitterly, and thought to himself that he had figured he would receive this kind of treatment from Mr Yeng, the man who boasted about being the representative of the poor. "My name is Sam, sir!" He reminded him about the past, "I was formerly the head of the labour union, and I helped with publicity for your excellency during the elections. You assured me that if I ever needed anything, I should come to see you at any time, your excellency. You guaranteed that you would help with any troubles faced by the poor, that you would be like our eyes and ears, sir…."

The representative of the poor smiled when he heard such florid words. "Oh! At that time, there were so many workers who helped and supported me, but after I was elected, I already repaid their kindness by giving them 200 or 300 riels each."

"Ah, is that right, sir?" Sam asked unhappily. "But I never received anything from you, your excellency. I haven't come here to cause trouble or to bother you, sir, about anything to do with money. I have only come to ask if I may please rent a *cyclo* from you, that's all."

"Yes, my friend! There is nothing stopping you," Mr Yeng replied immediately. "But I must hurry off to a meeting now, you see. You should go over to that side, and tell my secretary that you need to rent a *cyclo*. Tomorrow, you can bring 150 riels as a deposit, when you come back to take the *cyclo*."

Sam looked bitterly at Mr Yeng's face, and tried to smile through his disappointment. "Your excellency, sir! I have no money at all to pay you as a deposit, sir. Since I helped your excellency with the election publicity, please sir, won't you rent a *cyclo* to me just this once, without the need for a deposit?"

"No, I can't!" The people's representative interrupted, shaking his head. "I can't help you in that way. My *cyclo* are very expensive; if you have an accident with a car, or don't pay the rental fee for a few days, or throw away my *cyclo* and disappear, there would be nothing I could do about it!"

"But please, your excellency, be kind and remember that I used to help you, sir, and you promised that you would help me in return…."

"You idiot!" Mr Yeng shouted menacingly, and his face folded into a scowl. "You can't come here asking for favours like that. You already know that it was your duty as a citizen to help with the election. No one forced you to help me. And now you come here talking like an idiot! Get out of here! I don't need people like you."

"Your excellency!" Sam said, although he no longer had any respect or deference for him. "Now I can see clearly that we have been tricked and cheated by the likes of your excellency for more than a hundred years. The workers never receive any benefit at all from your excellency. In your election publicity, your excellency promised that you would represent the workers, and be like the eyes and ears of the poor. But your excellency has never done anything at all to struggle to ease the plight of the poor. And not only that. I came only to ask to rent your *cyclo*, and your excellency demanded a deposit, and also pretended not to recognise me…."

"Go away! Hurry up and get out of my house, go on!" Mr Yeng chased Sam away, while yelling at him threateningly. "If you still dare to speak to me like that, I'll call one of my people here to attack you right now. Do you realise you've made a big mistake here? You dare to come here and aggressively assault me, to come here and threaten and disrespect me! Careful or I'll call the police to come and string you up. Don't talk to me like that again!"

Almost before he'd finished speaking, Mr Yeng, the representative of the poor, went back upstairs into the house, in a furious mood.

In that moment, Sam felt he wanted to scream, to tell the world how stupid and ignorant the workers are! Oh! Every single time that there was an election, the workers, more than anyone else, would do everything they could to support and promote candidates who said they would represent them. But oh gods! Is there any candidate whose actions follow their promises? The workers and the poor are like tasty food for the hungry politicians. Before they're elected as the people's representatives, the workers and the poor do everything they can for them, even wiping away the sweat from the politicians' brows. But then, after they've been elected, those workers and poor are still in the same situation as before. Nothing has changed, and they never, ever see or hear anything from any of those politicians who campaign to lift the living standards of the workers and the poor. Most of the *cyclo* in the capital belong to foreign capitalists. The workers must sit on the seat and pedal, dripping in so much sweat that it becomes almost like drops of blood, but the money they make is only barely enough to survive and go on living as citizens. Despite the fact that the lives of the workers and the poor are so difficult, those politicians are never sympathetic or care to pay attention at all…. They only think of how to benefit themselves as quickly as they can, to enrich themselves. Oh, the politicians!

Chapter 13

Sam is Imprisoned for Being Homeless

The days and months continued to pass…. And the suffering and hardships of the workers who had nothing to depend on also continued to worsen with each passing day and month. Sam still looked for a *cyclo*, but he still hadn't found one, and so he had no way to earn a living. It was as if he'd been buried in a dark cave, without any hope. Now, Sam had become a homeless beggar. The owner of his small hut had evicted him, so he had nowhere to shelter from the rain and thunder, or from the heat of the sun. With no money for rent, Sam wandered the streets of the city aimlessly, searching for work. But everywhere already had enough workers.

One night, the skies opened up and drenched the entire city in rain. It was around nine o'clock, and Sam sat huddled under the eaves of the Wat Preah Puth Mean Bon temple, with two or three dogs sleeping nearby.[17]

By the looks of it, this pagoda seemed like a shelter for all kinds of pitiful and destitute souls. This evening, Sam had gone without food, because he had no money to buy any. He sat, thinking about his life and the terrible crises that he had met with. Fate had not helped Sam at all, and neither had any amulets or religious objects. Nature, which was usually a creative force for all people, seemed now as if it was only of use to the wealthy, and not to poor people like Sam. He had nothing of his own, except for the clothes that he was wearing.

Sam's musings vanished in an instant, when suddenly he felt a flashlight shining brightly in his face. Two police officers had come looking for him.

---

[17] Wat Preah Puth Mean Bon is a Buddhist pagoda in the north-western part of central Phnom Penh. Literally translated, its name refers to the virtuous or meritorious Buddha. Although it is a real temple, Sorin may also be using this toponym ironically.

"Hey, you!" one of them called out. "What are you doing sitting in the dark like that?"

Sam was not afraid at all, because he knew that he had done nothing wrong.

"Yes, sir!" Sam answered. "I'm sitting here to shelter from the rain."

"Well stand up, then," the other police officer said. "Where do you live?"

Sam realised that these police officers could accuse him of being homeless, and then arrest him and take him to jail. So he quickly answered, "In Toul Tompoung, sir."

The police officers checked in all of Sam's pockets, and then questioned him again. "You're near to Toul Tompoung already, so what are you doing sitting here? Come on, explain yourself!"

The look on Sam's face changed. He asked the police officers a question in return.

"What have I done wrong, sir?"

"There's no point in asking that. We asked you to explain yourself, so explain! You hear?"

The other police officer joined in. "We came to question you because we suspected you might have escaped from jail. I have the power to arrest you, and if I don't, you might go and rob someone. You have a very suspicious face, I can see that right away. If you try to resist, we'll put you in handcuffs right now!"

"Why do I have to go to jail, sir?" Sam asked angrily. "You think that any poor person wearing torn, old clothes and sitting in a quiet place must have run away from jail, or come to rob people? What about the people who drive cars, why don't you go and invite them to explain themselves, too? Do you suspect them of having escaped from prison, or of driving a car in order to go thieving, sir?"

"Eh! This guy's a smart one, that's for sure!" One of the police officers interrupted to say. "He can speak so sharply, just like a newspaper man, eh? Come on, quickly, let's not waste any more time. The government is implementing a programme to eliminate homelessness, you know!"

"In that case, why doesn't the government find jobs for the poor to do, sir?" Sam asked, unsmilingly. "And why doesn't the government find houses for the poor to live in, and rent them at a low price? Everyone wants a house and a job, sir."

One of the police officers lifted his hand as if he wanted to slap Sam, but he didn't dare to do so, because these days not many people dared to hit or kick anyone.

The other police officer grabbed Sam by the wrists, and snarled at him, "Eh, damn you! Don't talk so tough! Come on, let's go!"

Sam gritted his teeth, still enraged, but said nothing more. He followed the police officers calmly to the station as their suspect. Life for the poor is always like this; they must always put up with going quietly to jail, to show that they are good and well-behaved people. And then they must suffer in jail for a few days.

The police interrogation revealed no wrongdoing on Sam's part, and so two days after he had been taken to prison, the police commissioner released him. They told him to find a job, and that if he didn't, he'd be considered a vagrant, again, and they'd put him in prison, again.

"I'm out of options, sir," Sam explained to the police officer. "If your excellency has any pity for your fellow man, please take me on as a servant, sir. I will be delighted to repay your kindness to the fullness of my ability, your excellency. As for my wage, that's up to you, your excellency. Take pity, sir, and give me whatever you wish; I ask only to be able to live."

"I can't rescue you!" the police commissioner said gently, showing his kindness. "I also earn only a small salary, just enough to take care of my wife and children. I really pity you, but I don't know what to do for you. Don't be too disheartened; this is your fate, to be born as a poor person. Please, keep on striving…."

Wherever he went, Sam was trapped. People always screamed and chased him away, and with words that were grating to hear, just because his clothes were old and worn. Most important and wealthy people looked down on him and spoke to him harshly.

Chapter 14

Morality and a Plate of Rice

One, two, three days of suffering passed for Sam.

One day, he struggled with a thirst and hunger more mighty than any human could bear. There was nothing in his stomach but water. Every minute, his thirst and hunger increased; it made him light-headed, and he almost collapsed many times.

That night, while Sam was walking, he stood in front of a shop selling food in the Old Market.[18] He peered into the restaurant, and saw a group of four or five gentlemen eating together. The men looked very happy, and as Sam stood and stared at their mouths, he suffered. He was almost dead, as he stood there and watched them eat, and his face fell with sorrow and despair.

The force of hunger and thirst can force people to do anything, and to forget about morality. The force of hunger and thirst can change people, and make them do anything to try to stay alive, and escape from the grip of the devil. Sam cast his eyes toward the door of the shop, where there was a glass cabinet with chickens and grilled ducks hanging inside it. The sight made him lick his lips, with ever-increasing hunger.

Sam thought of going inside and sitting down in the restaurant, and ordering the Chinese to bring him all the food he could eat to satisfy his hunger. When he was full, he could sneak out of the shop without paying. Even if the Chinese tried to do something about it, Sam wasn't afraid. But when he looked down and saw how he was dressed, Sam changed his mind. There was no way the Chinese would make food for him, because his appearance and dress would be totally out of place in the restaurant.

---

[18] The Old Market, or Psar Chas, is located in central Phnom Penh, between Wat Phnom and the Tonle Sap River.

Suddenly, a fancy-looking gentleman walked out, with an aggressive air about him. When he saw Sam standing in the path to enter and exit the restaurant, the man stopped and shoved him in the chest, pushing Sam aside.

"Get out of the way!" the man said. "You look like someone who was born a beggar, huh!"

The man walked over to his American car, which was parked nearby, and the driver opened the door for him. Sam gritted his teeth and clenched his fists. He realised that his torn and loose clothing made people think he was a beggar, even though he had never begged anyone for anything, not even one cent…. Oh! People pay no heed to good and pure deeds. People only know how to measure the extent of goodness with gold and silver! They value only glamorously dressed and youthful people, and care not what terrible deeds those people commit….

"Hey!" Sam thought to himself, feeling furious. "I'm a good person, I've worked hard and strived to do good, but that goodness has never given me anything at all in return. I need to help myself for once, if I'm going to avoid death."

Hunger and thirst had forced Sam's heart and mind to transform completely in an instant. His eyes turned red and glazed, and he walked away from the spot where he'd been standing, until he reached the Dara cinema.[19] He looked defeated and despairing. In that instant, the film that had been screening reached its end. Crowds of people pushed past each other as they exited the cinema. Sam caught sight of a middle-aged couple among the crowd, who were also bustling out of the theatre. Both of them were modestly dressed, but in a way that showed that they were very wealthy.

The woman was slightly plump, and she was carrying a crocodile-leather handbag. In an instant, Sam resolved to commit an evil deed. He figured that inside that crocodile-leather handbag, at the very least there would be enough money to help him to avoid starving to death this once.

The power of lowly evil had been born in Sam's heart and mind…. He passed through the crowd until he was close to the couple, and then suddenly he snatched that crocodile-leather bag from the woman's hand.

"Help! Help!" the woman cried out. "Thief!"

---

[19] One of the dozens of cinemas in Phnom Penh at the time, the Dara Cinema was located opposite the National Museum and School of Cambodian Arts, on Street 178. Also known as CinéStar, it was regarded as a cinema for wealthier patrons.

Sam ran quickly into the National Museum.[20] He had risked being chained up in jail, all because of his hunger. Usually, when people go running, it is to compete against one another, in pursuit of a medal or reward. But Sam was running because he had stolen money to buy food. You could say that he was running to compete against dying of hunger.

This was the very first time in his life that Sam had committed an evil deed and broken the law.

People, including the police, had chased after Sam. He took a shortcut, running behind the National Museum until he reached the Arts School. The darkness there made it easy for him to hide, and the hairs on Sam's neck stood on end as he narrowly escaped arrest. He went to hide quietly in the covered hallway behind the Arts School, and then took the handbag and opened it wide, putting all of its contents into his shirt pockets. Sam threw away the bag, and then immediately walked away. He knew he had escaped safely when he had jumped the fence near the drain on the north side, and got away.

Sam was so embarrassed and ashamed of himself when he realised his terrible misdeed. Before, he had sworn to himself that no matter how poor he was, or how difficult things became, he was resolved to maintain his morality and not to commit evil. But now, Sam had become a thief, snatching a handbag, all because of his unbearable hunger. Those who have never experienced hunger and deprivation do not know how mighty is its power....

Sam tried to hurry as he walked away, and after a short while, he had arrived at the edge of the Old Market, which was filled with stalls at which Chinese and Vietnamese sold food, all arranged alongside one another. Sam went in and sat down in at a table in front of one of these market stalls, and then took out the contents of the handbag from his pocket to inspect. He was shocked when he saw more than thirty 100-riel notes, as well as seven or eight more five- and ten-riel notes, and many other things.

Sam called out to the Chinese to cook a plate of rice porridge for him, and to bring a glass of iced tea. The smell of the food in the Old Market was strong, and it tickled Sam's nose. He could hardly wait for the Chinese to bring him his plate of rice porridge. He ate it without a care for anyone. Because he hadn't eaten or drunk anything for the whole day, he thought that he would

---

[20] The National Museum of Cambodia was inaugurated in 1920, and holds a large collection of Khmer antiquities. The School of Cambodian Arts (later renamed the Royal University of Fine Arts) was built around the same time, inaugurated in 1917, in an adjoining location and with a similar architectural style. The site also adjoins the Royal Palace.

probably need five more plates like this before he felt full. He called for the Chinese to bring him another.

Sam's feeling of fatigue vanished, and he began to feel more and more energetic. He felt delighted with the gods and with all the magical amulets for helping to rescue him from being captured by the owner of the handbag or the police, and especially for helping to rescue him from dying of hunger.

Around twenty minutes after he'd devoured the second plate of rice porridge, Sam felt full and satisfied, and felt that he had truly escaped from death. He called for the Chinese to bring him some French cigarettes and matches, and he sat and watched the smoke drift away, as if he were watching himself relax, and watching his worries float off into the sky with the cigarette smoke. Sam thought of his friend Mey, who was lying sick on the floor mat, unable to do any work to support himself. After paying the Chinese, Sam took a *cyclo* and rode directly to Mey's house. While riding along in the *cyclo*, Sam again took all the things out from his pockets to look at them…. He saw a small bottle of perfume, and a box of face powder. But then, when he took out another box from his pocket, he was shocked.

Inside this small box, there were two diamond rings and a diamond pendant, shining brightly. Sam shut the box, and put it back in his pocket immediately. Sam had never owned a diamond in his life, but he knew that these were very valuable ones.

He realised that the gold and diamonds inside that box were worth many tens of thousands of riels, and that their owner must be crying with regret at their loss, and swearing about him in all sorts of curses.

Sam didn't dare to take out and look at anything else, but again and again he put his hand in his pockets to feel the things in there, and to make sure that nothing had fallen out.

When the *cyclo* arrived at the destination, Sam hurried inside the house to greet Mey. He saw him sitting in the doorway, looking sick, and holding his child in his arms. Mey called out in a friendly voice: "Eh, is that you, Sam? Come in, Sam, come in! Have you found a *cyclo* to drive yet?"

Sam went and sat down next to Mey, and said with a smile, "I'm still looking, brother Mey, but I haven't starved to death yet, which is my very good fortune." As he spoke, Sam peered inside the house. "And where has dear Mom gone, brother?"

"She's gone to sell cakes, and left the baby with me to look after." Mey took a long, deep breath. "None of us know what cursed, terrible fate is in store for us, Sam. You can't find a *cyclo* to drive, and I'm sick and can't go anywhere. Oh! But Sam, do you have any particular reason for coming to see me at night like this?"

Sam turned his head and looked around, and when he saw that there was no one nearby, he said: "Brother Mey! I've had some very good fortune, that has been born from a terrible action. Let's go and talk a bit inside the house, I have some big news."

After hearing only that much, Mey already knew that Sam had definitely committed an evil deed. He stared at Sam's face with a strange feeling in his heart, because he had thought that people like Sam hated and despised evil deeds more than anything. Mey turned to him curiously, and asked: "What's happened, Sam? Good fortune born of your own bad actions, eh? Come on, tell me what happened."

"Brother Mey, I know that you'll criticise me, for sure, because I've had to commit a terrible deed, for the first time in my life, in order to escape from death."

"Oh, dear Lord!" Mey said, with a trembling feeling in his heart. "No matter how poor you are, why didn't you come and see me, Sam? I told you already that you're welcome to come and stay with me. Why didn't you come here?"

"Brother Mey!" Sam said, with sympathy. "You want me to come here and bother your baby again? Oh, brother! It was hunger and thirst that forced me to steal. I shouldn't have done that, but I had to. What else was I to do, brother?"

"You stole!" Mey's eyes opened wide, and then he asked in a whisper, "Did you rob someone, Sam?"

"That's right!" Sam admitted. "I robbed someone near the Dara Cinema. I was almost dying of hunger, and then suddenly I saw a woman walking out of the cinema, and I rushed in, snatched her handbag, and ran away to the Arts School."

Mey sat and listened, feeling afraid for Sam. Sam reached into his shirt pocket, and took everything out for Mey to see.

"I still have everything that was in the bag, it's just the bag itself that I threw away."

"My god!" Mey cried. "This isn't a small amount of money here, Sam. My god, the owner has probably gone to file an official complaint already, I'd say!"

Sam took a bundle of papers and looked at them. "This is a receipt for the loan of 20,000 riels, and this is a receipt for a deposit on a house worth 100,000 riels. And that money, all together it's more than 3,000 riels." Sam's face was white with shock, when he thought of the loss that the owner of these things must be feeling. He lifted his head to look at Mey, and said, "Brother! All I needed was just one plate of rice. But that plate of rice cost the owner of these valuables great fury and a terrible loss.... So what do you think I should do to make it right, brother?"

Mey did not answer right away, but passed to Sam four or five name cards that had fallen out from some other papers.

"Sam, what can do you? It's up to you, you know. I don't dare to tell you what to do."

Sam looked quietly at the name cards, while he thought about how to rectify this situation. The name cards belonged to the owner of this property. The inscription was brief, and said:

Oknha Sambo Sambath[21]
123 Veradong Boulevard
Phnom Penh

"Brother Mey!" Sam said sadly. "I'm going to take all of these things and give them back to the owner now. I've spent only fifty riels of their money. I'm willing to accept my wrongdoing, and tell them the truth, that I only stole their handbag because I couldn't bear the hunger. If I do that, perhaps they will have some sympathy for me, and who knows, maybe they might give me a reward for doing the right thing, for knowing the error of my ways. But what do you think, brother, about me going to do that?"

"Oh, if that's what you want to do, that's good, Sam!" Mey answered, while looking at him intently. "But I won't applaud you, since this has come in a terrible way. The reason that I love and admire you, is because you are a worker who always follows the moral path, like me, Sam! I really do sympathise with you, and realise that you needed to steal to save your own life, and avoid starving to death. But I still don't understand. I'm your good friend, so if you were hungry, why didn't you come to see me? I still have enough rice left to feed you, too, until you can find a job, Sam! You should take all those things back to the owner, go on! Go now, Sam, go. I think maybe the owner won't cause any trouble; they'll be happy, and they'll love your character for knowing that you did the wrong thing. Perhaps they might even help to support you by giving you a job, or at least help to find a *cyclo* for you to drive, Sam."

Sam sighed, feeling both relieved and afraid. "In that case, I'll take all this back to the owner," he said.

---

[21] "Oknha" is an honorific title, traditionally bestowed by the King. It grants a noble status, and is considered a reward for meritorious service to society. "Sambo" and "Sambath" are both common names, but in this combination also carry a meaning of "great riches".

He wrapped the things up in a small cloth, to bring them back to the owner. Sam went down from Mey's house, having resolved to risk going to prison, since he knew he had done wrong.

Chapter 15

Sam is Imprisoned for Being Honest

The walk to find the house of Mr Oknha Sambo Sambath was not difficult at all, because all of the houses on Veradong Boulevard had individual numbers. Sam stood and hesitated in front of the gate, and peered into the house. The electric lights were still burning brightly, and there was a servant walking back and forth inside. The property was big and spacious, and the house was built in a modern and up to date style.

After standing and hesitating for a while, Sam resolved to go inside. He met a female servant as soon as he reached the foot of the stairs. Sam lifted his hands in a *sampeah*.

"Excuse me, miss! Are Mr Oknha and Madam here?" Sam asked in a very kindly and gentle manner.

"Yes, they're here! They only just got back home a moment ago. Brother, why do you need to see them?"

"Please miss, go to inform Sir that I have come asking to meet him on a personal matter."

"I think he probably won't see you," the servant said, while staring at Sam's face and his clothes. "He's very angry at the moment, because some gangster stole his wife's handbag earlier this evening."

"In that case, it's easy!" Sam said, and laughed. "Please miss, go in and inform him that I am the gangster who stole the handbag."

The servant stood, white with shock, and stared doubtfully at Sam. After a moment, she spoke. "Yes, in that case, it's easy! I'll go in and inform him now."

The servant hurried back up into the house. At that moment, Mr Oknha and Madam had just arrived back home from the police commissioner's headquarters, and were sitting and trying to calm down, feeling enraged with fury over the loss of their belongings. The woman-servant bowed down respectfully and approached them.

"Madam! The gangster who snatched your handbag is here now, and asking to meet you. He told me that he has brought all of your things back to you."

Mr Oknha and Madam seemed shocked. They had never heard of any thief like this, who brought back the valuables after he had stolen them.

"What did you say?" Mr Oknha asked in wonder. "The damned thief that stole our handbag has brought our things back?"

"Yes!" the servant answered. "He has brought your things back to give to you, and now is standing at the bottom of the stairs."

Mr Oknha and Madam jumped up from their seats, and hurried out to see Sam. Both stood and stared, inspecting him from afar. Madam imagined that she could still remember his face.

Sam bowed down respectfully, and lifted his hands in a *sampeah* to Mr Oknha and Madam from the bottom of the stairs.

"What's your name?" Madam asked him curtly. "Where do you live?"

"Please Madam, forgive me! Please, sir!" Sam answered with his hands still raised in a *sampeah*. "I'm the person who snatched your handbag."

"I know, because I remember your face," Madam interrupted to say. "But I want to know, what is your name? Where do you live?"

"My name is Sam, Madam."

"Your name is Sam," Madam exclaimed. "You don't look so bad, either. So why are you thieving for a living?"

"Your things are all still here, Madam!" Sam said, as he passed the belongings back to Mr Oknha Sambo Sambath. "I spent only fifty riels, and I had to throw the bag away, Madam."

Mr Oknha called for Sam to come upstairs, and he took his belongings and inspected them with his wife.

As soon as he saw that everything was still there, Mr Oknha smiled. But he turned and stared at Sam with a venomous fury. "That crocodile-leather handbag cost more than 1,000 riels. It's no joke, you know."

Sam tried to smile through his sorrow. "Please accept my apologies, Madam," he said respectfully, addressing them both. "I threw the bag away, because I was worried that I might get caught. I have taken this opportunity to come to inform you, and to accept that I have committed a grave wrong. I have never stolen anything before, Madam. I am a *cyclo* driver, but I can't find a *cyclo* to drive. Today, I had eaten nothing at all, because I had no money to buy anything. My thirst and hunger forced me to dare to take a risk, and steal your handbag, Madam, just to get some money to buy something to eat. I've hurried here to give it back to you, Madam. I hope that your excellency will take pity on me. I am truly very sorry…."

"Oh, this guy!" Mr Oknha said, overcome with laughter. "Your wrongdoing is very serious! I can't just overlook it. I almost can't bear to hear your excuse for your thievery, which you say was because of hunger."

The blood drained from Sam's face immediately on hearing this, because he had never expected that Mr Oknha would speak like this. Usually, people will forgive someone for committing evil, if that person accepts that they have done wrong. Such a person should be treated kindly, and be pardoned by the owner of the valuables.

Before Sam could say anything more, Madam called out loudly. "I am so sad to have lost that bag! Where did you throw it away, do you know?"

"No, Madam!" Sam replied. "If I knew where it was, I would bring it back to you, Madam."

Madam yelled out for one of her servants to come over to her, and instructed him to bring Sam to the police. Hearing this, Sam was terrified.

"This guy is the thief who stole my handbag. Take him to go and explain himself to the police. Careful, don't let him run away! I've taken all my things back from him already."

Before the servant and the driver of the car took him to the police, Sam prostrated himself in front of Mr Oknha and Madam, raising his hands in a *sampeah* and begging them to accept his apology. "Your excellency! Madam! Please kindly forgive me, this once! If you take me to the police, I will surely be imprisoned…."

"Oh, you realise that you'll be imprisoned, do you?" Madam said angrily. "If you're afraid of jail, then why did you become a thief? I can't accept your apology, that's up to the police."

Sam lifted his head to look Mr Oknha and Madam in the face out of the corner of his eyes, to show that he was begging them.

"Madam! Madam, you should pity a thief who knows that he's done wrong. Please forgive me, Madam."

"No! I have no pity for you," Madam said, shaking her head. "It is impossible for me to forgive a thief. You are a thief, you must go to prison." Madam turned to the servant and driver, who were standing nearby. "Go! Take him to explain himself. No more delays, eh?"

The word "prison" is a word that everyone is afraid of, and one that no one wants hear. Sam was afraid of prison, like anyone else. His pleas for forgiveness had vanished into thin air. Sam stood up, and laughed a little to himself in frustration.

"Madam!" Sam spoke in a normal tone now, not quite as respectful as before. "Now I can see clearly that doing the right thing is useless. If I'd known this before, I would not have brought all your things back to you. I thought that Madam might take pity on a thief who stole from you because he was hungry...."

Madam snarled at the servant again. "Go! Get him out of here!"

In that instant, Sam prepared himself to struggle with Mr Oknha Sambo Sambath's servants, and try to free himself. Bang! His right hand was ready, and he hit the driver on the jaw when he came to capture him, following Madam's orders. The driver fell to the ground. The servant rushed over to join in, and Madam and Mr Oknha called out for another person to come out from inside the house and help to capture Sam.

Then Sam, the unlucky worker who had admitted his wrongdoing, found himself surrounded by perhaps ten of Mr Oknha and Madam's servants, who punched and kicked him. Mr Oknha and Madam stood watching, afraid that Sam would get away.

He tried to struggle and run out of the house, but the servants had him surrounded on all sides, blocking his path. Someone's leg kicked Sam right in the stomach, with all his strength, and Sam collapsed. As he fell, the others kicked him as hard as they could, until Mr Oknha called for them to stop.

"That's enough! Any more and he'll die! And that will be trouble for me, eh. Well done! Lift him up and carry him off, go on, and I'll follow you soon."

Sam's entire body hurt. The servants grabbed him by the shirt and pulled him up onto his feet. His face was swollen, and his cheek and lip were bleeding. They dragged him away by force, without any pity or kindness at all.

Within an hour, Sam was in the police prison. No matter what happened, he was certainly going to be sentenced to prison as a thief, but Sam had accepted his terrible fate.

This was the punishment inflicted by the owner of those valuables, who had no pity or compassion for Sam's wrongdoing, even though he had admitted his mistake. This worker, with his terrible fate, was charged by the police as a thief, and taken to the court to be sentenced.

Sam pleaded guilty to all the charges against him, without protest. He informed the judge that the only reason he had stolen the property was because of hunger. He only asked the judge to be compassionate, and pleaded with him to reduce his sentence a little.

It seemed as though after hearing this plea, the court was sympathetic. The judge sentenced Sam to six months in prison.

Once again, Sam walked into Phnom Penh's Kuk Thom prison.

* * *

Days and months passed by with great difficulty for Sam. He suffered in both his body and his mind. This time, life in the Kuk Thom prison was different than before. None of Sam's friends came to visit and ask after him. He was made to do hard labour, and to eat just four or five mouthfuls of disgusting food each day, in order to survive. After six months in the Kuk Thom prison, Sam had lost a great deal of weight, and by the end he was almost unrecognisable.

Sam gritted his teeth and tried hard to persist and endure his sentence. He didn't complain about the hardships in Kuk Thom. And finally, his beloved freedom was returned to him.

One morning, the deputy director of the prison called for Sam to go and meet him. He told Sam that he would be freed, because the court had issued a decree ordering his release. "Prisons were created as places to put immoral and terrible people. Prisoners are all evil people who have committed crimes," the officer explained to Sam. While he spoke, he was smiling brightly, and it seemed as though he was delighted that Sam was being released. "You must return to being a good citizen from now on, and don't act out of turn. I bless you with good fortune, and I hope that from now on all will be well and good for you. And I hope that I never see your face here again…."

"Indeed, indeed!" Sam lifted his hands in a *sampeah* gesture while receiving this blessing of good wishes. "I consider this to be a great grace, beyond all expectations, that your excellency has kindly reminded and encouraged me of this, and blessed me with good fortune. I am firmly resolved to be a good citizen, from now on."

Chapter 16

A New Place to Depend On

After leaving the grounds of the Kuk Thom prison, Sam didn't know where to go. He had no house, and he had no money. He wandered aimlessly down many streets, and felt hopeless.

After a while, Sam decided to go into a trading business. He headed directly toward a middle-aged man, dressed in lavish clothes, who sat working at a desk.

"Please excuse me, your excellency!" Sam said, while lifting his hands in a *sampeah*. "Do you need any coolies here, sir?" he asked respectfully. "I've come in search of a job, your excellency."

The man glared angrily at Sam, as if he had been his mortal enemy for the last thousand years. "Who let you in?" he screamed. "Get out of here! You look like a beggar, and you're stupid enough to come looking for a job!" He rapped loudly on the table. "Hey, secretary, chase this idiot out of here!"

Sam tried to smile through his sorrow. "There's no need to chase me out, sir. I'll leave now. I've only come here to ask for a job, and nothing more, because I'm destitute. But if your excellency won't give me a job, then I'll leave, sir."

"Go! Get out of here! And don't talk so much. I don't have any job to give to you. Whether you're rich or poor, why do you come here and make it my responsibility? That's your problem."

The poor, hungry worker gritted his teeth, and walked sadly out of the shop. Oh, what a pity! The two men were both Khmer, just the same! They were like brothers: both were human, just the same! It's not right that anyone should be so hateful or mistrusting like that.

The sultry afternoon sun blasted its ever-increasing heat…. Sam had walked in all directions along the streets of the capital. He sat down to relax under the shade of a tree, feeling exhausted. Sam's stubborn determination not to go to ask for help from Mey, his old friend the worker, was now melting away. He saw that he had no one else at all to depend on in times of difficulty, other than Mey. So he decided to go and see him again.

But when he arrived at Mey's house, Sam saw that new people had moved in. The neighbouring house, which four or five Khmer workers used to rent, had now become a house full of Chinese and Vietnamese. Sam saw an old lady sitting selling cakes under a tree nearby, and asked her what had happened. She stared at him, and then shook her head while she answered.

"Oh, you're asking about Mey and Mom? They left more than a month ago, my child. The landlord came and asked them for 500 riels to repair the house. But Mey didn't have the money, so the landlord evicted them, and now he rents the house to Chinese. They paid him 1,000 riels in 'tea money' as a bribe, and the monthly rent is 300 riels. It looks like this neighbourhood is now almost completely Chinese and Vietnamese, my child, because they can pay the 'tea money' as a bribe, you see."

"Oh, Grandmother! People worship money like it's a god!" Sam sighed. "It looks to me as though it won't be long until we Khmers all run off to the countryside, and leave the marketplaces to the Chinese and Vietnamese," he said with annoyance. "The landlords are all looking for ways to evict the Khmers, and rent the houses to Chinese and Vietnamese so that they can take their 'tea money'."

After Sam left the area near Mey's old house, he continued to walk aimlessly, drifting, a worker who couldn't find any work to do. And finally, inevitably, he began to starve again. He wasn't going without food because he was on strike, to demand his rights and freedoms. Sam was just hungry because he had no food to eat.

Like a corpse moving all by itself, Sam could not stop walking, wandering and drifting aimlessly. His face became dark and discoloured, and his eyes dull and lifeless. His clothes and frame were no different from a beggar's. From noon, through the afternoon, and into the evening, Sam's thirst and hunger tormented him. He had consumed nothing but some water from the side of the road to soothe his dry throat. He was depressed and defeated, and his whole body was withered and weak.

One evening at around half past five o'clock, Sam received a terrible shock. He had been crossing the road, with his mind in the clouds, and hadn't seen a car that was coming right at him. The driver slammed on the brakes to try to stop, but he still hit this poor, hungry worker. Sam collapsed in the middle of the road. Two or three women screamed, after seeing what had happened.

This kind of accident might be considered terrible luck for a wealthy person, but it was also good luck for a poor person like Sam, because this accident was the reason he found a job. The young gentleman who was riding in the back seat of the car was a government minister. He had recently returned from France, a year earlier, and had just been appointed as a minister a few months ago. Feeling afraid, and pitying poor Sam, the young officer opened the door of his car immediately, and went to look at what had happened.

The driver rushed to lift Sam up in his arms, but the accident had not been too serious. Sam's right knee was grazed, and his leg was sprained, but that was all. The government officer helped Sam to stand, and then inspected him carefully and sympathetically.

"Lift him up into the car," the government officer instructed his driver, "and bring him to the hospital." Then he asked Sam, in a kindly tone, "How are you, brother? Where are you hurt?"

"Don't worry, sir!" Sam answered, in a small voice. "It's nothing serious, and it's my fault, for walking across the road so carelessly, without looking to the left and right first. Please, your excellency, kindly let me go. My wounds are only small, so there's no need to go to the hospital, sir."

"Well, in that case, I'll bring you back to your house," the government officer said with a smile. "Where do you live, brother?"

"I don't have a house, sir," Sam answered sadly, and in a respectful tone. "I'm homeless and alone, a worker without a job, sir."

The young government officer nodded his head with pity while he listened. He was very impressed by Sam's modesty and gentleness. He saw that even though Sam was poor, and wasn't nicely dressed, he behaved and spoke in a lovely way.

"Brother!" the government office spoke in a sweet and friendly tone. "I really pity you, for having an accident with my car. I'd like to give you 500 riels for your damages, and if there is anything that you need, please come to see me." He handed the money to Sam, along with his name card. "Please do come and see me, brother."

The kindness of the government officer's words made Sam admire and respect him very much. He lifted his hands in a *sampeah*. "Your excellency, please don't give me any money, sir. Please, your excellency, it would be better if you could help me to find a job to do instead, because I'm searching for work. I'll do any job, too, sir, as long as it's honest work. I can do anything, and I don't mind if it's heavy work…."

"I'm a government official, not a businessperson, but I would be delighted to do everything I can to help you, brother. I need to bring you to the hospital first, and then I'll bring you to my house. You really don't mind about what work you'll do?"

Sam tried to smile, even though his body ached. He was absolutely delighted. "I am not fussy, sir. Tell me what to do, and I'll do it, as long as it's honest work."

The car drove slowly away, and Sam sat next to the government officer, in the back seat. The man looked at Sam, while his thoughts wandered. They were driving toward the Preah Ang Duong Hospital.[22]

"Brother," the officer said to Sam as they drove, "I'll let you be the caretaker of my household. It is a job for you to do, and it's not difficult."

"I'm so grateful, your excellency," Sam answered with his hands lifted to *sampeah*. "I'll do anything you wish, sir."

"We all need to be able to depend on each other sometimes, brother," the government officer said, while looking at Sam. "We must have equal rights and freedoms, but those rights and freedoms must have a limit. I'm so pleased to be able to help to support anyone who is suffering hardship. Sorry, brother, what is your name?"

"My name is Sam, sir."

"Do you have any brothers and sisters? Are your parents still alive?"

"No, sir."

"In that case, it's easy. I'll help to make your life comfortable. I don't need anything other than your honesty and integrity, brother."

"Yes, sir! I will be your servant, your excellency, and I will always be honest."

Sam's life had taken another turn, as was his destiny.

His health improved, and so did his happiness, under the shelter of the young government officer's house. The man was so generous with everyone.

---

[22] Preah Ang Duong Hospital is located on Norodom Boulevard in the city centre.

Chapter 17

The New Peasant

Because Sam had behaved so humbly and politely, the government officer took great pity on him, and cared for him very much. Sam took shelter under the government officer's roof, and lived very happily and well there.

But Sam saw that living as a worker in the capital was not comfortable and enjoyable. It was not a living filled with honour and glory; not a living that had any prosperity or growth at all. Living in the city these past few years, Sam's life had been gradually devastated, like a flower without enough water, withering and fading day by day.

When Cambodia gained its national independence, because of the royal achievements of His Majesty Samdech Norodom Sihanouk the King— achievements that shone so brightly on the pages of Khmer history—the entire kingdom, which had suffered such terribly perilous insecurity because of those barbarians, now had been transformed into a truly peaceful kingdom.

All classes of the Khmer people, both in the city and in the countryside, had also received tranquillity and happiness, without fear of further insecurity.

Sam saw that there was one crucial factor that could lead people's lives in the right direction for prosperity and happiness in future. It was the rice fields, which were so vast, but had no one to plough and tend to them. There were fields in Sam's home district, in Battambang province, that could become a source of great mountains of wealth, if only there were peasants who would work hard to clear them, plough them, and tend to them anew. It was most regrettable! It was regrettable for the bright fields that were a legacy that the Khmer ancestors had built and kept for future generations. And Sam had cast aside this most essential thought, for many years now!

But this wasn't because Sam was afraid of honest, hard work. When he'd left behind the countryside to come to the city, it had been to labour in jobs that drenched him in the sweat of hard work. And to make a living from physical labour in the city had made Sam increasingly destitute, much more than in the countryside.

Sam had left the countryside because of the insecurity.

Now, a new sun has risen over the old land—has risen over the land of French colonialism, has risen over the deceitful politicians. A new sun has brought brightness and peace and showered it over the old land!

Sam resolved that he must return to his place of birth, and plough the fields like before....

He was overjoyed when he remembered his life as a peasant in the past, a life which was filled with freedom, happiness and harmony. He resolved that he must return to that life again.

Sam still remembered that on one blessed day, His Royal Highness the Father of National Independence had royally decreed to his fellow compatriots that they must remember the rice fields, for those rice fields are the basis and foundation of the national economy.

Sam was delighted with that royal decree, because he understood that the Khmer rice fields were like gold and jewels, for a flourishing economy. And so, because he was a patriotic Cambodian citizen, Sam decided that he must return to his homeland in the countryside, in order to cooperate with his fellow Khmer peasants to rebuild the basis of the economy, that had been weakened and fallen into decline during the era of colonialism. They must make it great and strong once more.

Sam would bring a harrow, a hoe, a spade, a scythe, a sickle, and all the tools of his new livelihood, and he would rush to build the life of "the new peasant".

And just as he had planned, indeed Sam went back to his life as a farmer, with a happy heart. But after three years of farming rice, he still hadn't achieved a good return, because his fields depended on the skies.... If the skies delivered rain, then Sam and all the other peasants would have hope, but if the skies were dry, then the life of the peasants would suffer and wilt like the skies, too, without any hope. Sam, like most Khmer peasants, farmed the rice fields with very little yield at all. And so Sam, like other peasants, fell into despair and hopelessness.

But their despair would not last for much longer. No, not at all! The peasants would be overjoyed once more. Now, the life of the peasants that had before been filled with suffering and decline, was filled with a fresh joy and happiness, and a new hope.

What was the source of Sam's hope? Was it the hope of an agriculture that depended on the skies?

No! Sam could stop placing his hope in the skies.... Now, Sam could depend on the "water policy" instead.[23]

Since the period of the Sangkum Reastr Niyum[24] had begun, under the brilliant and clear leadership of His Majesty Norodom Sihanouk, Cambodia had taken a very large step toward a new era, "the era of building".

The Royal Government had helped to improve the lives of the population in every way, especially through "yearly plans", which included a programme concerning manual labour: the heart and soul of the peasants.

These days, Sam no longer placed his hopes in the skies, for he had a water dike, a reservoir, a well, and enough water. Before, he used to make offerings and say prayers to the spirits to bring rain ... but now, even if there was no rain, Sam had no need to despair. His land, which had never before had a water dike or a reservoir or a well, now had become a great store of water.

The Royal Government of the Sangkum Reastr Niyum had led the population in the construction of many dikes, and the digging of many reservoirs and dams in Sam's province. All the peasants in the area, including Sam, had been delighted to work hard and contribute to this building effort.

All the peasants, including Sam, were no longer worried and fearful about a shortage of water for agriculture. In particular, Sam's rice fields, which had yielded such poor crops in the past, now reaped great rewards for this new peasant....

Sam was very satisfied with this "water policy", which involved the building of dikes that were beyond comparison. Sam's fields profited, and so did the fields of the other peasants, too. Rice fields in every part of the countryside across the entire kingdom prospered, and when the agriculture profited in this way, the national economy also flourished.

Other than this, the Royal Government of the Sangkum Reastr Niyum has assisted the peasants in other ways, too. They have promoted the nation's agricultural produce, which has given Khmer products a solid reputation for high quality, both within the nation and in foreign markets, too.

Sam had no need to worry about a shortage of water for irrigation, but also no need to worry about a shortage of crops, or about destructive insects or other pests....

---

[23] "Water policy" (*nayōpāy dyk*) was the term used by Norodom Sihanouk and his government to refer to the development of irrigation infrastructure for rice agriculture.
[24] Sangkum Reastr Niyum was the name of Norodom Sihanouk's political organisation, which ruled Cambodia from 1955 to 1970. The term is also used to refer to this period. It is usually translated as "People's Socialist Community".

These days, in Sam's province, just as in every part of the kingdom, the Royal Government had created a Ministry of Agriculture. It served as a model for peasants, both for methods of planting crops, and also of storing and protecting agricultural products. Sam had received training from the Ministry in every related field, including fertilising the soil and making the crops robust and productive. Sam was happier with his work than ever before.

Once, pests attacked Sam's rice crops, and those of his neighbours. Sam called on the Ministry of Agriculture to help to combat the insects, and the Ministry appointed an agent to take action, spraying pesticide like Sam had requested. Sam saw clearly with his own eyes that the current age was the era of building under the Sangkum Reastr Niyum, not at all like during the French colonial period, or the period of false independence.

During the era of the Sangkum Reastr Niyum, the Royal Government had intervened to help the peasants with their agriculture, and had also elevated the status of the peasants, to be valued citizens in the national society. The peasants in the era of Sihanouk were not debased like in the previous eras.

Sam loved the Sangkum Reastr Niyum as much as life itself. These days, he offered his respect and blessing to the Sangkum Reastr Niyum with all his heart.

He had seen clearly with his own eyes that His Majesty the Father of National Independence was not elitist. He often went out to join in manual labour himself, and he had love and sympathy for the common people.

Under the Sangkum Reastr Niyum, every government officer must throw down his pen, once in a while, in order to take up a hoe, a spade, a scythe, and farm alongside the common people. This is in order to teach them to understand in their hearts and in their minds about the lives of the common people.

Sam believed that in the pages of Khmer history, there had never been a king or any other hero who had gone out to do manual labour with his own hands, like His Majesty Norodom Sihanouk. Recently, His Majesty the Prince had even gone to do manual labour with his own hands in Sam's own province, nearby to his village. Sam loved the Sangkum Reastr Niyum with all his heart, because he saw clearly that the brilliant and clear leadership of His Majesty Norodom Sihanouk had certainly brought great benefits to the population. Sam joined with the other villagers, volunteering to help with the hard work, as he understood and loved manual labour.

Sam offered all his physical energy, and all his heart, to the Sangkum Reastr Niyum, without any thought for his exhaustion. Before long, the villagers in Sam's province all knew and loved him, and listened to his suggestions, and considered him their leader.

Because of Sam's dedication to the nation, religion, and king, and his efforts in all kinds of work, and because he had led his fellow countrymen to perform the manual labour that is necessary to achieve the goals of the Sangkum Reastr Niyum, the Royal Government was very impressed by Sam. They praised him, and offered him a supreme medal.

Before long, the people in Sam's province elected him the Party Chief for his commune in the Sangkum Reastr Niyum.

After his election as Party Chief, Sam worked harder than ever. He led his villagers to follow the policies of His Majesty the Royal Comrade, such as to love their work, and to join together and cooperate in the digging of reservoirs and wells, and also the building of roads, bridges and schools. In addition, Sam encouraged the villagers to love their civic duties, not to behave dishonestly, and so on.

Most especially, Sam taught the villagers to understand the importance of the National Congresses. Whenever a Congress was held, the villagers came in large numbers to join.

The people in Sam's village used to be ignorant and stupid. Now, they were educated, and they understood their role. In the past, Sam's province used to suffer from famines, but now it had become a place of happiness and plenty. The people there used to be destitute, and now their lives were more easy and comfortable than most....

Chapter 18

Modern Phnom Penh

The train had arrived to the Phnom Penh station…. The passengers were all very happy to have arrived safely to their destination. It was twelve o'clock. The station was very busy today, much more than usual, because many people had gathered here while they waited to greet their relatives and friends who were visiting the capital in order to join in the Ninth National Congress, which would begin tomorrow. The sound of their voices echoed through the station as the passengers all rushed to hop off the train.

Once he was off the train and had walked out of the station, Sam hailed a *cyclo* to bring him to his accommodation, at the Lumhae Aakas Hotel.

Within a moment of setting foot in Phnom Penh, Sam could see that the capital was much more crowded and busy than it had been seven or eight years earlier. There were cars, bicycles and *cyclo* along every road, and the traffic was never-ending, but the city was also very neat, orderly and well-organised.

That evening, Sam rode a *cyclo* to look at the city's sights, which were like the face of the nation. He could see clearly with his own eyes that within the last few years, Phnom Penh had changed a great deal indeed. There were many more houses and other buildings, and these were much taller than before: as much as seven or eight storeys high. There were many more cinemas, and almost all the roads had been widened. Many neighbourhoods which before had been almost completely unchanged, now had roads, running water, and electricity. A beautiful monument had risen in place of the former Koun Kat Bridge, which before had been a foul-smelling place. The monument's fine decorations were no different from those at Angkor Wat. It was a memorial for Independence….[25] Sam travelled from this new monument, and saw that from

---

[25] The Independence Monument was designed during the late 1950s by architect Vann Molyvann, under instructions from Norodom Sihanouk. The various other locations named in this chapter all refer to actual places in central Phnom Penh.

the east of the Psar Kab Ko market all the way to the Wat Keo temple, now had all been modernised. There was a dike road from the Monivong Bridge all the way to the Yamareach Bridge, which was four kilometres along the road to Kampot. Before, this had been such a quiet place that no one would dare to travel there alone, but now it had a beautiful road, and many houses that had been very well built, and quite close together. Sam travelled along Monivong Boulevard, and saw that the area to the west of the Psar Thom Thmei market, which before had been filled with nightclubs and small thatched huts, and had been a haven for prostitutes, now was filled with hotels and other very big, tall buildings. Further to the west was Chamkar Chin, which in the past had been a farm belonging to the Chinese, in which there was a bad smell and it was very easy to get lost. Now it had become a residential neighbourhood, which also had big, tall buildings. The Prek village had been home to prostitutes and gangsters in the past, but now had become the Royal School of Medicine, which was part of the Calmette Hospital. And Wat Phnom, which used to be a place where thieves and gangsters defecated and waited for people to rob, now had become a place for people to take a breath of fresh air, and enjoy the cool evening breeze.

Along the riverside, Sam saw a shelter for labourers. When he reached the Wat Preah Puth Mean Bon temple, he saw a shelter for *cyclo* drivers, and the people living inside all looked remarkably happy.

Sam felt great regret…. Regret for the time when he had become a worker, seven or eight years earlier, and had no one to depend on, no shelter, when he had lived on the streets and slept under a tree…. Now, the workers in the new era had achieved their great destiny, which was provided by the generous hospitality of the Royal Government. They had been rescued, provided with a place to live, a place to shelter from the rain and from the heat of the sun.

Sam saw many other marvels, too, that had appeared during the era of the Sangkum Reastr Niyum. He saw a great many primary schools, elementary schools, secondary schools, and universities which had taken the place of the nightclubs that had been there seven or eight years earlier. There was the Preah Mohaksat Treiyani Kossamak Hospital for Buddhist monks, the Khmer-Soviet Friendship Hospital, clinics in every neighbourhood, and maternity hospitals, as well as every other kind of modern establishment. The old hospitals left over from the French colonial period, such as the Preah Ket Mealea Hospital, had been very beautifully renovated.

Public roads and public health had been greatly improved in the present era, because the Royal Government had devised strategies for safeguarding the health of the population. Sam saw that they did not allow the people to be impoverished and embattled like they had been in the previous era. The

Royal Government had established a generous programme to give the poorest sections of the population dependable healthcare. What's more, Sam saw that public health had been greatly improved in the countryside throughout the entire kingdom, just as in the capital.

Seeing all of this, Sam felt great regret.... He felt regret for when he had been a worker in the city, with no hospital he could rely on. Now all the people had dependable care. Sam felt terrible regret for the death of his wife.... Regret for the time, seven or eight years ago, when the common people could not depend on a hospital. Perhaps if it had been like nowadays, his wife would not have died, and would have lived to see the many great advances of her nation.

Sam saw that there were more and more modern cars, of every kind. At night, he saw the electric lights burning as bright as day. Along every street, and in all the big shops and cinemas, there were electric lights in red, blue and yellow that enchanted the eye.

All of this made Sam realise that Cambodia was progressing very well, in all regards. Many nightclubs had been wiped out. Sam could still remember them clearly from seven or eight years ago, the time before the country had achieved independence. Back then, Phnom Penh had been packed with nightclubs, like the Cooperative Bar, the Himalaya Bar, the Khochnil Bar, the Intersection at Night Bar, and so on. Now, in the new era, nearly all these nightclubs had shut their doors, and there was only a small number remaining. There were also not so many bars for music and dancing.

This showed Sam that Khmer citizens of every class had nowadays changed their attitudes. They had done away with fun that wastes time and money, for no benefit, and instead thought only of working hard, in order to contribute to improving their nation.

Sam respected and followed the leadership of His Majesty Norodom Sihanouk, the Father of National Independence.... He also concluded that in the era when the country had been under the control of the French colonialists, all the power had been in the hands of the deceitful politicians, and government officers who committed mostly immoral acts.... And so they found it easy to make a lot of money, which they then threw away at the nightclubs, wasting it on Cantonese women and mixed-race women, without any sense of regret. The nightclubs were in fierce competition, and they popped up everywhere, like mushrooms.

And so in today's era, why have those nightclubs closed their doors? Who forced them to close?

Sam himself could see the answers to these questions. He concluded that ever since the nation had gained independence, the Royal Government of the

Sangkum Reastr Niyum under His Majesty's brilliant and clever leadership had worked with all its might to benefit the motherland. The Royal Government had struggled to improve the lives of the poor and lower classes in every way, passing strict laws that decreed that government officers at every level must not abuse the common people, must not take advantage of them, rape them, or commit any other immoral acts. By creating a ministry to clean up the dishonest government officers, the Royal Government had stopped the abuses of previous generations. Now that the officers were no longer dishonest, they were no longer spending their ill-gotten gains in the nightclubs, and no longer spending their money on Cantonese or mixed-race women. The government officers now earned only enough money to support themselves and their families. The nightclubs had no customers, and so they themselves decided to close, without anyone forcing them....

* * *

That night at the Lumhae Aakas Hotel, Sam lay and pondered the many kinds of progress in the kingdom, that had been delivered by the Sangkum Reastr Niyum under the lovely leadership of His Majesty, the great commander of the Khmer nation.

Sam thought of the agenda of tomorrow's National Congress.... Section 12 of the agenda had caught his attention the most, it was a request from the residents of Kampong Speu province.

Sam was very disturbed by this request. In this age, every class of the Khmer population was joining together in order to build the motherland. It wasn't right that some people should promote themselves or think only of their own benefit....

Chapter 19

The Ninth National Congress

It was eight-thirty in the morning already.... The morning sun shone brightly, and the sky in the east was bright blue, like the colour of a heron's eggs. Members of all the different Congresses had joined together in the Veal Preah Man royal field.[26]

By this time, the party officers, members of both the Senate and the royal family, and the government representatives had all arrived. Then, His Majesty the Prince and the Queen Mother also arrived.

His Majesty the Prince by his Royal Decree declared the proceedings to have commenced. He then welcomed all the congressional members, with his charming and affectionate smile. His Majesty described the nation's successes in every political sector, both nationally and internationally, which were the results of the nation-building work of the Sangkum Reastr Niyum since the Eighth National Congress. The congressional members listened carefully, paying close attention. His Majesty explained that the progress of the nation since the previous National Congress was due to the great achievements of the Sangkum Reastr Niyum. He then described these accomplishments, as follows:

The Five Year Plan has established factories for manufacturing paper, factories for manufacturing utensils, and factories for manufacturing plywood. The Plan has also established the Khmer-Soviet Friendship Hospital, and created organisations that cooperate with the government in order to properly gather, monitor, and distribute the goods and

---

[26] Located adjacent to the Royal Palace in central Phnom Penh, and in front of the National Museum and Arts School, the Veal Preah Man royal field is an open garden, traditionally reserved for royal-religious ceremonies on Cambodian Buddhist holidays. Under Norodom Sihanouk's rule, it also became the location for political gatherings, such as the National Congresses described here.

equipment that the Royal Government receives from our many friends internationally, as well as those that we have produced ourselves. In the field of education, we have provided support and assistance to youth with a technical inclination, and as a result we have opened the door for their future careers. New kinds of employment are open to them, which will benefit the nation and also the youth. Before, many youth were in a difficult situation or else were adrift without any support. The national financial reserves had previously been depleted by private interference and graft. Under the Five Year Plan, ideas have been gathered for increasing the speed and expanding the volume of national production. Water has been managed so that Phnom Penh now has a sufficient supply. A festival has been held to celebrate the opening of the Khmer-American Friendship Highway. Construction has begun on a large bridge over the Tonle Sap River. And the runways have been lengthened at the Pochentong airport.

A beautiful lighthouse has been built for ships travelling in Koh Rong, with the assistance of the French; a hospital with twelve beds for the Royal Khmer Armed Forces has been built in Phnom Penh, and a ceremony held to inaugurate it. Universities of science and literature, as well as a Khmer-English university, have been built. A canal has been built in the Siem Reap Baray reservoir, with American assistance. Several dikes and dams have also been built.

His Majesty described the nation-building progress of every sector in the various ministries, and he concluded by observing the following points:

In the time between the Eighth National Congress and the Ninth, many important events have taken place in Cambodia as a result of cooperation. This shows us, increasingly clearly, the strength of our nation's solidarity and neutrality. Now, a terrible hurricane could not topple us. Fate has brought our nation to a situation of rapid progress and cultural modernisation.

Another important event has been the treason committed by groups of Khmer traitors, who have betrayed their own nation. In addition, there have been the malicious actions of various foreign governments. They have promoted, expanded and accelerated the Khmer national independence, peace and unity, which are based in neutrality, our defence against annihilation—but they have done so only in order to make us slaves, to divide us from one another, to create anarchy and insecurity and then to take our land and spread a terrible war.

But the fruit of the virtuous deeds of the spirits, and the triple gem of Buddhism, together with the patriotism and solidarity of our nation's people, have defeated our enemies and prevented them from destroying Cambodia as they planned.

Because of our good fortune, we have had the opportunity to continue building our nation, allowing it to progress in every domain.

His Majesty also declared that we must succeed in our quest to quash corruption, swindling, thievery and other forms of profit from the nation and the Royal Government.

Finally, His Majesty shared his great fear about the development of international affairs in our region of the world.

The instability in our neighbouring countries is increasingly serious. We worry that this spark of insecurity may spread, and in the near future could start a fire under the roof of our own house. What's more, some foreign governments—despite the escalating problems in their own countries—have been shouting denouncements. They want their allies to hear them, and to believe that the atmosphere of increasing turmoil here is dangerous for their countries. This means that now it is essential that the name Norodom Sihanouk is synonymous with Khmer neutrality.

Along the horizon of our nation's future, there are dark, black clouds. They make us worry that we may no longer have enough peace and security to build our nation and allow it to progress. For the dangers that we face are not only on one side; they may hit us from both directions. Both blocs seem intent on escalating the Cold War, and continuing their secret and silent war which takes place within our national borders, without any respect at all for our sovereign rights or our neutrality.

They have persecuted me excessively over our neutrality, and over the harmonious relationship between our nation and the socialist countries, especially between our nation and the People's Republic of China. I have endeavoured to calculate: if we were to agree to forgo our neutrality and enter into an alliance with the Western countries, alongside Thailand and other nations, would our population be pleased and benefit from this, or not? After careful consideration, I see only one answer. No! It is clearly impossible. We would be completely destroyed!

In short, we see that Cambodia has but one possible path to follow, as a strategy to protect the purity of our independence, our solidarity and our nation, and in order to avoid the terrible disaster that would annihilate forever our nation and its place in the world. That path, that strategy, is neutralism.

In conclusion, His Majesty called upon and roused the nation's citizens, who are like his children, to tighten our ranks and unite together more strongly than ever, and do whatever is necessary for our motherland to continue to live with honour and freedom.

The members of the National Congress listened intently….

Next, His Majesty announced the occasion for the National Congress to engage in discussion, one by one. Each member of the Congress used this forum to offer their opinions and advice about the nation's most serious concerns, in the most honourable manner.

Sam, like every other member of the Congress, was overjoyed with the warm and welcoming atmosphere of this Ninth National Congress.

The members carried out their duties for three and a half days. They encouraged each other to share and discuss their opinions, and to tirelessly offer solutions for all the major issues, for the great benefit of the nation.

Conclusion

The train steamed quickly away from the Phnom Penh station, and headed toward Battambang with a thunderously loud sound.

Almost all of the passengers today had come to join in the Ninth National Congress, and were now travelling back home. Sam, too, was travelling back to his province.

He sat and smoked a cigarette, and cast his eyes over the landscape alongside the train tracks. His mind wandered happily....

Sam thought of the past. He thought of the progress of the nation in the present. He thought of His Majesty's speech, which had been delivered with his magnificent smile.... He thought of the grave problems facing the nation, which the National Congress had discussed.

Sam was overjoyed with the progress in every sector throughout the kingdom. He was determined to continue his work as a peasant, because agriculture was also helping the nation to prosper. He also resolved that he would try to find a way to come to join in the Tenth National Congress, too.

All along the way, on both sides of the train tracks, the landscape was filled with great fields of golden rice, ripe and ready for harvest: a peasant's delight.

Sam looked at all this nature; it prospered because of the work of the peasants. This nature seemed very happy with the work that the peasants were doing. Their work allowed it to flourish over this old land. In times past, this old land had been wilted and despairing. It had been without the light of the sun, and without any thought of growth. Now, a new sun shone its light on that nature. This was the brightness of the growth that was being built by all the peasants, and by His Majesty Samdech Norodom Sihanouk, the Father of National Independence and the most marvellous leader.

Sam thought of the Khmer people, of every class. Regardless of what anyone thought, Sam still believed that *a new sun has risen over the old land.*